TERROR IN TUSCANY

THE CIA CONFRONTS THE MAFIA IN WINE COUNTRY

LARRY ANDREWS

ACKNOWLEDGMENTS

My wife Sue for always being there

Bob Conger for Intelligence Agency insights

Eddie Bay for initial manuscript editing

Millie Ames Writer's Workshop for the critique during
manuscript development

Jeff Guenther Author's Conservatory for book development
and promotion consulting

CONTENTS

CHAPTER 1

In Transit

*A*s they approached the door of the condo Marcus said, *"Remember, Jenna, Angelina said it will be dark, and you have to flip the light switch just inside the door on the left."*

"I know, I know," said Jenna as she slid the key into the lock, pushing the door slightly open. It was pitch dark inside. Jenna carefully put her hand on the wall to the left feeling for the light switch.

"I think you are a little high," said Marcus. "Move your hand down a little."

"I've got it." said Jenna.

BOOM. *The room exploded.*

"No!" screamed Marcus.

"Marcus are you all right? Wake up," said Leo.

At this point the flight attendant arrived asking, "What seems to be the matter?"

"Nothing really," said Leo, "my partner here fell asleep and was dreaming."

In a cloudless sky after clearing the Alps, the British Airways Airbus 319 was descending on approach to the Venice airport. Leo had been engrossed in an Italian travel guide that he had been studying during most of the two-hour flight. Marcus had fallen asleep shortly after takeoff and, from his facial contortions and body movements during the flight, had been in a deep dream. Waking up with a start and seeing the flight attendant and Leo staring at him, he shook his head a little and said, "It happens all the time. I fall asleep and immediately recall the disaster that occurred back home."

"What disaster? We have been working together for about three months now and you really never told me about your background and how or why the CIA sent you over to work with MI6. I have been on this drug issue for some time. How does this affect the US?"

"I'm sorry, Leo. I thought you would've been briefed before I arrived. My last assignment involved a Mafia crime boss in New York. We determined he cut a drug deal with the Calisto cartel in Colombia. It appears now that an organized crime syndicate, the Gambioni Family, has drugs on the street but the FBI has not been able to determine how they're getting them into the country. They suspect that they might be coming in by way of Europe. Hence my assignment with MI6 is to see if your drug issue could be related."

"Wait, that's all fine but . . ."

"Fasten your seatbelts, bring your seatbacks to a full upright position. We will be landing at Marco Polo Airport shortly," came the announcement over the PA system.

"What about the disaster? Where does that fit in the picture?" continued Leo.

"It's a long story and I'd really prefer not to get into it now, maybe sometime later. Now Leo, back to our assignment. With little warning, you stayed late at work last night, came home and told me to pack as we were going to the airport this morning and flying to Venice. What's going on? What's in Venice?"

Recognizing that Marcus appeared to be sensitive about his past assignment, Leo immediately switched back to their current mission.

"Look, Marcus, in MI6 when you're told to do something or go someplace, you just do. We are scheduled to meet with an Anti-Mafia Investigation Department agent at Harry's Bar at four this afternoon. Supposedly we both will be briefed then. Now you know as much as I do."

"Leo, I've never heard of Harry's Bar and I know nothing about Venice. In fact, this is my first trip to Europe."

"Not to worry, Marcus, this will be a great adventure. I have been in Italy many times and will certainly enjoy being your tour guide. Let's be off."

Claiming their bags and exiting the Marco Polo airport, Marcus was surprised to see that to the right of the terminal was a huge body of water.

"Wow, Leo, we could have arrived by seaplane. I guess I was sitting on the wrong side of the plane because I didn't notice this at all when we came in for a landing," said Marcus.

Leo ushered Marcus in the direction of the water saying, "This is the Venice lagoon and Marcus, you're in for a real blast."

While they were walking towards the lagoon and chatting, they were not at all cognizant of the meeters and greeters taking pictures of arriving passengers.

"They let me pick the hotel," continued Leo, "as long as I stayed in the price range required, so we are off to the Hotel Violino d'Oro. I stayed there once with my girlfriend and it's a great little hotel and a perfect location. It's just off the Grand Canal on the canal San Moise and will be just a short walk to Harry's Bar and St. Mark's Square. The water taxi is the fastest way to Venice proper. They race like a speed boat across the Venice lagoon, but immediately slow down to a crawl when they enter the grand Canal. You're going to love Venice. I just hope we get to stay here for a while, there's so much to see and do."

The water taxis were no different than cabs. They were all queued up along the dock and you were supposed to jump into the first one in line. As they handed their bags to the driver and hopped aboard, Leo said, "Hotel Violino d'Oro, *per favore*."

"*Si*, please sit and hold on. I speak and understand English. Most all do as it is a required second language in school now. Would you like a tour? I can do that for 150 euros. Otherwise, it will be 70 euros to your hotel."

"Hotel *per favore, grazie*."

With that the driver pushed the throttle full forward and Marcus and Leo fell into their seats as the boat went up on plane. You could have water skied behind the taxi as it sped across the Venice lagoon toward the Venice island cluster and the entrance to the Grand Canal. Marcus was surprised when the water taxi pulled up to the side of the canal San Moise and they were literally just feet away from the hotel entrance.

"Well, this has got to be a first," said Marcus. "I don't believe I've ever heard or experienced door-to-door travel, airport to the hotel, by boat. You promised an adventure and it sure has started out that way."

◉

On check-in they were happy to find their rooms both had access to a small patio on the top floor of the hotel. This provided an excellent view of the canal they had arrived on and the bridge intersection on the street to Piazza San Marco. Stepping out on the patio and looking down, Marcus said, "Look at all the gondoliers. Do they always hang out here?"

"Yes, this is one of the main pickup spots for renting a gondola. If you look down the canal, you will see all of them lined up. You probably didn't notice them this morning when we checked in as most of them weren't here or those that were, were covered up and tied up to the side of the canal back a little way. They normally don't start renting until midmorning to early afternoon. If we get some time, we'll go on a gondola ride. You get to see parts of Venice that you can only see from the water.

Look, it's almost 4:00 so let's hurry. It's just a short walk to Harry's Bar."

"Why do you think the Italians picked Harry's Bar? And by the way, what is Harry's Bar?" asked Marcus.

"They did not know what hotel we were staying in. I'm sure they picked the place because it's a tourist stop and it would be easy for us to find. But quite frankly, you wouldn't find it by yourself without asking someone or knowing where it is. The entrance is on a side street and somewhat obscure. It's a small place inside and supposedly used to be a hangout for Ernest Hemingway and the like. It has an interesting history. I was curious and looked it up when we got our assignment."

"Oh really, tell me more."

"Seems it was opened in 1931 by a bartender, Giuseppe Cipriani. According to the company history, Harry Pickering—a rich, young Bostonian—had been frequenting Hotel Europa in Venice, where Giuseppe Cipriani was a bartender. Pickering suddenly stopped coming to the hotel bar, and when he did show up, Cipriani asked him why. Pickering explained that he was broke because his family had found out his drinking habits and cut him off financially. Cipriani loaned him 10,000 lire. Two years later, Pickering returned to the hotel bar, ordered a drink, and gave Cipriani 50,000 lire. 'Mr. Pickering, thank you,' he said, and before he could say another word, Pickering handed him another 40,000 lire saying, 'This is to show you my appreciation. Now go open a bar and let's call it Harry's Bar.

"I learned this all on the Internet. It further related that Cipriani later opened several other venues in Venice, Paris, and I believe in the UK and US. I'm not sure how many of them still exist as I understand he had some tax issues in the US that caused him to sell some of them.

Harry's Bar is famous for the Bellini, a drink of prosecco and peach nectar. It's called a bar, but it's really a restaurant. However, the food they serve is very expensive, so don't get carried away if the Italians want to eat. It could kill our expense account."

"Wow, Leo, the adventure continues."

Following a short walk to St. Mark's Square, they made an immediate right down a small alley towards the Grand Canal. Just before the canal there was a door on the left that said, Harry's Bar.

"I see what you mean, Leo," said Marcus. "You really have to know where it is to find it. The alley is not necessarily a main thoroughfare. St. Mark's Square is really huge. After our meeting I hope we can get back and do a little exploring."

"Oh, definitely. We will walk through it as research for our restaurant for tonight," said Leo.

As they entered the bar, they were startled by hearing their names called. "Agents Harris and Peterson, over here," came the call from a table in the corner immediately to the left of the entrance opposite the small bar. Seated at the table were three men neither Marcus or Leo had ever seen before.

"Please sit," said the man in the center. "I am Agent Toscano from DIA." Nodding his head to the right, he said, "This is Agent Rossi, GF," and nodding his head to the left, "and this is Agent Romano, CSA. Welcome to Venice." Then looking at the waiter who had appeared as soon as Marcus and Leo sat down, he said, "Bellini, *per favore.*"

With a surprised look on his face Marcus said, "I don't understand. For a famous tourist spot, this place is quite empty."

"It's four o'clock," said Agent Toscano. "We picked that time for good reason. This is a tourist stop and from 11:00 when it opens till about 3:30 or 4:00 it's a zoo with tourists. After 4:00 most all tours are over and the tourists either go back to their hotels or the cruise ships that brought them. It quiets down until about 5:00 when the locals and regulars come.

"Now back to business. Let me explain. Our law enforcement agencies are a little different than yours. Agent Rossi's organization is responsible for financial crimes, smuggling, money laundering and illegal drug and people smuggling. Agent Romano is from the Directorate of Anti-drug Services, obviously the fight against drug trafficking. As for myself, I'm from the Anti-Mafia Investigation Department and I'll be your main contact.

"Now to the case and why you were summoned here. We, specifically, my department, have been tracking the Sicilian Mafia in their drug operations. And they continue to be quite ingenious on how they get the drugs into this country. But that's another issue. Based on some of the shipments we intercepted and comparing that with what appears to be available on the street and Interpol's estimate of what exists coming into France, we came to the conclusion that a sizable amount is coming into Italy and then leaving for somewhere. We suspect either the UK or the US. How? We have no idea. In communication with both your agencies it was felt to be beneficial to all to have representation in our investigation. You both, obviously, are that representation."

At that point the Bellinis arrived and were set before everyone at the table. Agent Toscano raised his glass and looking around said, "Again, welcome to Venice and here's to a successful investigation." Then doing what appeared to be a strange thing, Agent Toscana took his cell phone out of his pocket and after making a few clicks, faced it toward Leo and Marcus.

"Wow, that's a picture of both of us," said Marcus. "How did that get on the Internet and what does it say underneath?"

"Unfortunately, you will find the Mafia is quite capable and provocative," responded Agent Toscano. "This is one of their websites we monitor on the dark internet and the caption below your picture says, 'Welcome to Italy, Agents Harris and Peterson. We hope you survive your visit.'

They obviously know who you are and suspect what your mission is. I don't believe there is any immediate danger for either of you, but they protect their operations at all costs. So always be on your guard."

Trading cell phone numbers, Agent Toscano indicated that some local raids were being planned in the area and Marcus and Leo should stay available as they would be contacted to participate. The game plan was to follow local sources to see how distribution was flowing up from Sicily or wherever. Past raids had revealed that drugs, primarily cocaine, were coming into the country via Sicily but other ports of entry were suspected.

Parting company as they left the meeting, Marcus said, "Leo, you can go on and check out a place to eat as we planned earlier. I have to get back to the hotel and skype headquarters in New York. It's about

11:00 in the morning and they will be expecting an update from me on our operation."

"Good thought, Marcus. I will check out some of my old haunts and get back to you on my cell."

Marcus rushed back to the hotel and set up his laptop on the marble-top desk in his room. He was surprised at the speed of the internet. Bandwidth was much better than what he had experienced in the UK. The skype call should be no problem, he thought.

As the call connected, he could not believe the face and voice he heard and saw on the screen.

"Hi, Marcus, how are things going?" she said.

Here speaking to him was a colleague he had worked with on his first operational case. He had last seen her when she was in the hospital with a completely bandaged face suffering from severe wounds resulting from an explosion they had both been involved in. That happened months before his assignment to the UK. The relationship he had had with her on their last assignment flashed into his brain, and passionate feelings began to overtake him. "Jenna, is it really you? You really look great. How come you are answering my skype call?"

"Thank you. It's good to see you too. As you can see, I am completely healed and back to work. I have been assigned as your contact for the Mafia drug case. They thought since I had worked the Gambioni case earlier with you, I would be the logical agent here to be your interface. What's your status?"

He suddenly realized he still had strong feelings for her. Quelling these, he gave her a full report of the meeting they had just had with the Italian law enforcement agencies and further indicated that he could be involved in their future planned raids on the local Mafia drug distributors.

"Marcus, be careful. By the way, there are other CIA operatives working in that part of Europe who could be called upon if absolutely necessary. Their missions and locations are naturally classified but knowing of their existence should boost your confidence."

I'm glad I didn't tell her about the Mafia knowing I'm here and possibly tracking me, thought Marcus. He then responded, "I assume you are my contact if I need any support."

"Yes, and I will give you my cell number that you can call 24/7 if needed," responded Jenna.

After trading cell phone numbers, they agreed there would be a skype call after any operation, otherwise weekly.

After ending the skype call, and after seeing Jenna and hearing her voice, Marcus realized he still harbored a strong attraction for her. *I best put any thoughts of that on hold until after this operation,* he said to himself.

CHAPTER 2

Welcome to Italy

Later that evening Marcus and Leo toured St. Mark's Square and ultimately had dinner in a small restaurant just off the square. Arising the next morning, they had a leisurely breakfast at the hotel and were first in line to catch a gondola. Leo instructed the gondolier to take them on a grand tour. The gondolier smiled and they could see the euro signs in his eyes as he graciously accepted the order and they took off.

They were on the canals well over an hour or so with the gondolier announcing and giving the history of several sites. Marcus was extremely interested when he talked about the Bridge of Sighs and asked, "Do prisoners still go from the Doge's Palace prison to the Inquisition rooms across that bridge?"

"No, Marcus, that was back in medieval times," said Leo.

"How do you know so much about Italy?" asked Marcus.

"My father's English but my mother's Italian and very proud of her native country. So naturally I had to learn about it. I also had to learn to speak Italian. I don't let onto that, as it's fun and interesting to hear what the Italians are saying about us when they don't think we understand."

"And the gondolier, he is so knowledgeable."

"Gondoliers in Venice are considered professional and they are members of an exclusive guild. They have to take a rigorous exam that includes Venetian history and foreign language skills as well as practical oaring maneuvers on the canals."

They had just gone under the Rialto Bridge and the gondolier had given them its history when Leo's cell phone went off.

"Hello. Oh hi, Agent Toscano. We are on the Grand Canal at the Rialto Bridge. Yes sir, we can do that. We are on our way."

"We are on our way where?" asked Marcus as Leo put his phone away.

"Gondolier, we will get off here *per favore*. We must catch a water taxi," called Leo and then looking at Marcus he said, "That was Agent Toscano. An American tourist overdosed on cocaine and is being treated at the Ospedale SS Giovanni e Paolo. He wants us to meet him there. If and when they can bring her around, he wants to question her as to where she got the cocaine. He also will talk to the attending physicians to see if they can determine the strength of the drug that she took. It's really quite close and a water taxi will get us there in minutes."

"Why does he think we should be there?"

"Well, he thinks she would talk to us a little more freely than speaking to him. Americans are pretty cautious when speaking to foreign police officers, especially if they think they're going to be arrested."

The water taxi ride was in fact a really short trip even though it transited through several canals. As it stopped before a canal bridge leading to a small square and they both debarked, Marcus looked around and asked, "Where's the hospital?" They were facing a large gothic building resembling a church.

"Marcus, you're looking at it," said Leo. "Wait till we go inside. It used to be a 14th-century monastery. It was completely redone inside as a major hospital. If you had looked past the bridge, you would have seen the emergency boats further up the canal from where we got off. It's actually considered the place to go for emergency critical care."

Entering the hospital, they immediately saw Agent Toscano coming across the reception area to greet them. "Please follow me," he said as he led them into an adjoining visitors area. It was empty and as he gestured them to be seated, he said, "Unfortunately, it is a very sad situation. They were not able to bring her around. Her traveling partner was quite broken up but I was able to speak to him."

"Were you able to find out where they got the cocaine?" asked Leo.

"That's the interesting but very sad part of the story. They have been traveling in Italy on vacation and drove into Venice from Florence yesterday. He swears to his knowledge she had never taken a drug in her life. They have been going together for two years and last night he proposed to her at a small restaurant here in Venice. He prefers beer and she is a wine enthusiast. She was drinking some wine that they had purchased in Florence and became deathly ill. It was not until they got to the hospital that he found out she was suffering from a drug overdose. The doctors advised him that there was an unbelievable amount of cocaine in her system."

"How is that possible?" asked Marcus.

"Well, that's the interesting part. They evidently pumped her stomach when she arrived and in testing the food, they discovered that the wine contained cocaine."

"Cocaine in wine? Where did they get the wine? What was the label?" asked Marcus.

"All he could tell me was that while they were staying in Florence, at the suggestion of the hotel they were staying in, they took the number seven bus to the top of the mountain overlooking Florence. There they had lunch at a hotel restaurant that included a recommended wine. She liked it so much they wanted to get some and the hotel told them they could purchase it across the street in a small wine shop, which they did."

"I'm no expert on drugs, but is this the new way of getting a high, having it in wine?" said Marcus.

"Well, it was back in the 1800s," responded Agent Toscano. "It started with a French potion called Vin Mariani, which was French

Bordeaux infused with cocaine. It was quite popular among royalty and Pope Leo XIII awarded a Vatican gold medal to Angelo Mariani for producing it. But that's not what we have here. We are talking about copious quantities of cocaine infused in the wine for smuggling purposes and extracted out at a destination for distribution. I believe that bottle of wine was never intended to be sold in a shop."

A smile appeared on Leo's face and nodding at Agent Toscano, then looking at Marcus, he said, "Marcus, you're going to love Florence."

"*Grazie,*" said Agent Toscano. "I have an agent in Florence who will work with you. I'm not sure whether it will lead anywhere but it's worth a try to follow up on where the wine came from."

⊕

Somewhere in the hills of Tuscany at a large winery owned and operated by a family with possible Mafia ties, in the bottling and shipping shed, the following took place:

"You what! You took a bottle of the special reserve from the 'For external shipping only' and placed it in a local distribution case?"

"I am sorry. I was short one bottle and the shipment had to go out. It won't happen again."

"No, it won't," and then a gunshot occurred.

⊕

The Santa Lucia train station, located on the Grand Canal, provided for a relatively short trip by water taxi from the hotel. After checkout and a quick breakfast, Marcus and Leo were able to catch the 9:30 train to Florence. Settling into their seats, Leo said, "Marcus, it will only be a little over two hours to Florence on this express train. Had we had some more time, we could have taken the intercity train that stops at Bologna. It's a great little city, sort of a college town. Has great restaurants. Maybe on our way back."

"That might have been nice but the sooner we get to that wine shop in Florence, I think the better our chances of finding out about the wine. Did Agent Toscano give you a contact for us to use there? Since our primary mission is intelligence, I have to assume if we run into any difficulty or crime, we have to rely on local law enforcement. We have no authority here."

"You are right about that and he did. I have a cell phone for an Agent Lombari who we should contact on our arrival. In addition, he told me we would be joined by an Italian Interpol agent from Rome."

"What's that about?"

"They are investigating the flow of drugs into France and want to be aware of our findings. Again, as in your case, they believe this all could be connected."

"Did you get a name? and where will we meet?"

"Yes, it's an Agent Bufalino. She supposedly will meet us at the hotel. In fact she picked the hotel and made reservations for us. It's the Hotel Mario's. Agent Toscano told her about the wine and she, knowing Florence, picked it because it was close to the train station."

Marcus's face lit up and a huge smile appeared as he said, "You won't believe this, but she was involved in the Mafia/Colombian Cartel case I told you about. The one on the Caribbean cruise. Very attractive, and a sharp agent. Typical Italian, I mean that in a positive way, very friendly. She was undercover as part of the ship's shore excursion staff. Great to work with and I'm sure you'll like her."

The interior of the Florence Santa Maria Novella train station features a dramatic metal and glass roof with large skylights over the main passenger concourse. The skylights span the passenger concourse without any supporting columns. This gives a feeling of openness and vast space as passengers exit the trains and walk to the entrance.

Marcus pulled both their bags as Leo was on his cell's GPS app entering the hotel address. They approached the entrance when a loud scream echoed across the hall. "Marcus, Marcus!"

This was immediately followed with a beautiful dark-haired woman emerging from the crowd, who threw both her arms around Marcus, giving him a very passionate kiss.

Completely surprised and caught off guard, Leo looked on and said, "I understand this must be Agent Bufalino."

Marcus broke free and smiling, said, "Leo, may I introduce you to Martina Bufalino, Interpol, and Martina, may I introduce you to Leonardo Harris, MI6."

"Glad to meet you, and Marcus, so very glad to see you again. Agent Toscano told me the train you had planned to take so I picked the Rome train that I thought would get in at about the same time. It worked. Now just follow me," said Martina. "The hotel is just around the corner."

As they exited the station, Marcus was surprised to see all the local buses parked immediately in front but before he could comment, Martina, pointing at the first bus in the queue, said,

"That's the number seven bus that goes up to Fiesole, the village that steals the hearts of many locals and tourists alike. Its hillside location provides great views of Florence. Right after we check in, we will be on it." And, looking at her watch, continued, "We should be able to catch lunch at the hotel that the American tourists visited."

"I can't wait. Your romantic description is so enticing," said Marcus.

"Oh, there is more," continued Martina. "Across the street from the hotel is a site of preserved Roman ruins that includes an amphitheater that is still used today for summer shows."

All conversation ceased as they reached the hotel and checked in.

The number seven bus wound its way up the hillside, leaving Florence and ascending to the so-called Florentine Hill Station, Fiesole. History reports that it was the summer escape for the Romans from the hot Arno river valley. Exiting the bus in front of the Villa Fiesole hotel, they were surprised to see the small crowd across the street and an ambulance and police car. As they walked across to investigate, they were almost run over as another patrol car arrived.

"Martina, what's going on?" asked Marcus, not understanding a word of what was being spoken by many in the crowd. She walked into the crowd and got in conversation with one of the bystanders while

Leo said, "From what I'm hearing there has been some sort of a shooting."

Martina quickly returned saying, "Someone killed the shopkeeper. Evidently a patron entered the shop around noon to purchase wine and found the purveyor on the floor in a puddle of blood. I'll go speak to one of the officers."

Flashing her ID, Martina went up to the officer who appeared in charge and got into deep conversation. They were joined by the two plain-clothes officers who had just arrived and after a few minutes, she motioned to Leo and Marcus to approach. "Their English is not that great so I'll fill you in," she said as Marcus and Leo joined the group.

"It appears the shopkeeper was shot but no shots were heard by anyone in the adjoining shops. Obviously, some sort of weapon with a silencer was used, which is typical of Mafioso executions here in Italy. There is very little traffic up here but someone said they saw a nonlocal young man on a red Vespa around 10:00 this morning going into different shops and then leaving in a rush. Could have been the assailant. Not enough of a description to follow up on."

"I assume this was probably the wine shop the Americans bought their wine in," said Marcus.

"I'm afraid so," said Martina. "It's the only wine shop in this small community."

"Then I believe our only hope of finding where the wine came from may be the hotel," said Leo.

"They probably bought their wine here," said Marcus. "In a small community like this everyone usually patronizes each other. But if they know the name and/or have another bottle with a label, we should be able to trace it to a winery."

At this point one of the plain clothes officers pulled out an ID and said, "Scusate, I didn't introduce myself. I'm Agent Lombari. You are obviously the agents that Agent Toscano told me about. I suggest you continue your wine search on your own. We have a murderer to deal with. I have your cell phone, Agent Harris, and if anything comes from our investigation, I'll contact you. Again, if you should need my help locally, please call."

With that said, Marcus, Leo, and Martina politely withdrew from the group and exited the crime scene, Martina saying, "I don't believe we are considered welcome participants in their local murder investigation. Further, in true Mafioso fashion the assailant would have no idea of who called for the assassination. I suggest we continue our investigation over lunch at the Villa Fiesole hotel."

⌾

The hotel's veranda provided a great view of Florence proper and both Martina and Leo were quick to point out different sites to Marcus that are famous for the city.

"Oh, you are really going to like Florence, Marcus. We will have a grand tour this afternoon," said Martina, "but first we must continue our search for the wine. I'll question the staff while you both get seated for lunch."

Marcus and Leo were still perusing the menu when Martina returned looking quite happy.

"Oh, we are in luck," she said. "The staff, actually the manager, remembered the American couple and the wine they liked so much. He thinks they still have a couple of bottles left of it and is looking for it. He also remembers sending them across the street to purchase it. I did not think it wise to fill him in on the details so I said we had spoken to them in Venice and would be very interested in trying it ourselves."

"Great move, Martina. Whose expense account are we putting lunch on? MI6 doesn't go for alcohol," said Leo.

"Not a problem. I've got it. We Italians would not think of eating without wine," responded Martina.

The wine appeared. Marcus took a photo of the label and it was opened. Martina tasted and approved. They toasted and settled down for an enjoyable lunch. As they ate, Marcus and Martina reminisced over the activities they had shared on the Caribbean cruise. This delighted Leo as he learned details about the cruise and the case that he probably never would've heard from Marcus.

The afternoon was spent giving Marcus a grand tour of Florence, hitting the main spots such as Michelangelo's statue of David, the Duomo and Baptistery, Piazza della Signoria and Ponte Vecchio. The latter is referred to as the golden bridge due to the many shops featuring gold jewelry. Their tour included climbing up the narrow steps to walk around the Gothic dome that graced the Duomo. Dinner at a restaurant recommended by the hotel and early retirement concluded a very active day for the threesome.

The following morning their world changed. After morning pleasantries at the breakfast table Marcus and Leo were stunned at Martina's change in demeanor when she said, "Gentlemen, our mission has changed. I have been in conversation with my agency in Rome and Agent Toscano in Venice. The issues we are about to deal with concerning the wine's origin are somewhat complicated by the issues we have to deal with concerning you."

Looking at Marcus, she continued, "Marcus, there appears to be a mark on you floating around Mafia circles, suggesting your demise might be appreciated. It's not clear why, but I wouldn't doubt it might be emanating from the Gambioni syndicate in the US. If it is, the good news is, based on our Caribbean endeavor, we can probably assume the supplier is the Calisto Cartel in Columbia. The receiver in the US would be the Gambionis. A little more research will be required to validate this. However, as such, and since neither Leo nor myself seem to be associated with this mark, we are to do what we can to change your identity."

"Well, that's an exciting development and it doesn't necessarily give me a warm feeling," said Marcus.

"What about the wine? Were you able to find out anything about the winery from the label?"

"Yes, it appears to be a winery in Tuscany northeast of the small walled town of San Gimignano, which is a very picturesque village. I have been there. Its church and its little plaza is quite popular for weddings and it also is a popular destination of cruise ship excursions that include the Leaning Tower of Pisa just south of there."

"Gosh, I have been all over Italy and never got over there in my travels," said Leo.

"Cruise ship excursions?" asked Marcus.

"Yes, Livorno, just west of here, is a popular cruise port. It affords a variety of shore excursions in the area, and that brings me to our mission. Agent Toscano feels it would be best if the winery were investigated unofficially before an official raid was organized and implemented by the Central Directorate for Anti-drug Services."

"And I assume we are the designated unofficial investigators," said Leo.

"Well, yes," said Martina and her face lit up with a big smile as she continued. "In my sleep I came up with a great idea, and getting on the internet this morning, I was able to validate its possibilities. Serendipity has played in our favor. Marcus, remember that the Golden Duchess was due to transition to Europe after our cruise. Well, it is still here." Then looking at Leo, Martina quickly said, "We were on the Golden Duchess cruise ship on our Caribbean cruise assignment."

"Now you are going to tell me she is coming to Livorno?" asked Marcus.

"She is, day after tomorrow. She is in Barcelona today, Marseille tomorrow, and then Livorno. If I can contact the shore excursion staff, maybe I can arrange for us to be part of any excursions they have planned in Tuscany and near San Gimignano. That could allow us to arrive at the winery as part of a typical tourist group."

"Sounds like a great plan, but what are we to do with our Mafia fugitive?" asked Leo.

Martina picked up her handbag and retrieving a small package, said, "I thought about that and did a little shopping this morning." Unwrapping the package and passing a bottle of hair dye over to Marcus, she continued, "We are going to take care of that beautiful blond head of hair you have and you are about to be married again. This time to me instead of Jenna. As you are aware, married couples are the norm on cruise ships." Then looking at Leo, she said,

"Oh, there are occasional bachelors so you will fit in, but our Mafia fugitive here will be transitioning from a blond single American to a dark-haired married tourist, hopefully dropping him off the Mafia radar. By the way Marcus, no more skype calls to Jenna. The Mafia has ways of tracking them. All communication with your home office should be by email or a secure telephone service."

Martina, assuming the leadership role of the three, continued to bark out orders. "Now we have lots to do to carry out this plan. I will try to contact the ship and also the tour bus operation in Livorno. Leo, could you call and check with Agent Toscano? Apprise him of our plan and get any feedback. Marcus, time to get into character, hair and eyebrows. Let's meet back here and compare notes before we check out, say, in about an hour and half. It's an hour and twenty-minute train ride to Livorno on a direct run and they run fairly regularly. We should be able to get there by early afternoon."

They all arrived back at the hotel breakfast room together. "Marcus, you look great," said Martina. "With the dark hair slicked down, you almost look Italian."

"You do look different," said Leo. "Agent Toscano liked your plan, Martina, but with a slight change." He looked at Marcus and continued, "He would prefer we split up: one of us going to Livorno and getting on the ship's shore excursion with the other going to San Gimignano. His thoughts are that spending some time in San Gimignano, we might be able to accomplish some sleuthing on the winery. Their wines are probably sold there and he is sure that some of their workers probably live there."

"Great idea and that will work out well with what I accomplished," said Martina. "I was not able to get in touch with the Golden Duchess but I did get hold of the tour operation that will be conducting their shore excursions out of Livorno. Remember, Marcus, on our last operation, I was undercover as a shore excursion guide. Well, that's where I got my training, and while there I made some friends with the management. They indicated that the Duchess Cruise Line has booked a tour to San Gimignano and the winery in question. In fact, the excursion includes a wine tasting at the winery. Knowing I was an Interpol agent and when I explained our plan, they suggested that one of us go along as an apprentice tour guide." Looking at Leo, Martina continued, "I mentioned you. Being English and speaking Italian, they thought you would be perfect. In fact they were a little curious on how spoken Italian would sound with a British accent. They have accommodations in their Livorno facility for their tour guides. Depending on languages needed for excursions, many guides are not locals and need to be put up. So they should be able to take care of you. I would suggest you get the next train to Livorno as we had originally planned for all of us. That should get you there in plenty of time to check in before they close down for the day."

"Obviously, I don't have a vote in this but I agree it makes sense. We can't let our Mafia fugitive here wander around by himself," commented Leo.

"I'm afraid not," continued Martina. Then looking at Marcus, she said, "We don't have much of a choice. We either rent a car or take the bus. I suggest we rent a car. Can you handle that?"

"I don't think that's a problem at all," said Marcus. "I don't have any limitations on transportation expense. Besides, it could be fun driving on these Tuscan roads through the vineyards and olive groves. Maybe we could rent a Ferrari or Lamborghini?"

"Nice thought, but the tab on one of those I don't think would fly on any of our expense accounts. Remember, we are a young Italian married couple. Currently one of the most popular cars in Italy is the Fiat Panda. I'm sure that's what will be available at a reasonable price wherever we rent. It's a small four-passenger car and quite fun to drive. I have an older model at home in Sicily. Further, thinking about it, it will be better if I rent it. We don't want Marcus Peterson to exist officially any more. You never know who has Mafia ties.

"Now back to San Gimignano. Having been there, I suggest we stay at the hotel Leon Bianco. It's right in the middle of the walled town, right on the square. Great location, and reasonable price. Oh, I will also do the check-in there. You don't speak at all when we check in. I will be flashing my Interpol ID and signing the register. As far as the hotel is concerned, we are Signor and Signora Bufalino. That way they probably won't ask for our passports - again, part of keeping you under the Mafia radar."

Listening to all this, Marcus's mind began to spin. *This could get interesting,* he thought. *Martina became quite affectionate on our last operation when she found out Jenna and I were only posing as a married couple. Staying with her has some interesting possibilities.*

His thought process was broken when Leo jumped into the conversation. "Hey, it looks like you two are going to have all the fun, while I spin my wheels in Livorno learning to be a tour guide."

"Oh, I am sure you will have some adventure in Livorno," said Martina. "I didn't mention but you are going to be teamed with Sofia. She is a local girl, educated in France, who speaks five languages. She actually gave me my tour-guide instruction. Oh, and she is quite attractive and I'm sure will be willing to show you what Livorno has to offer while you wait for the Golden Duchess.

"Now back to the game plan. Tour buses are not allowed in San Gimignano due to the narrow streets. There is a separate parking lot just outside the wall for tour buses. On a normal day, that parking lot is filled and in constant movement: buses coming and going, unloading and loading. It can be an absolute zoo. We will have to communicate by cell phone so that we can meet your bus and become part of the group.

"Now, the other issue is that tours sometime go to San Gimignano before a winery tour and sometimes after. Sofia said she would try to do San Gimignano first but it won't be decided until the day of the tour. The issue is determined by the wineries as a function of what they have individually scheduled. There are overland bus tours that also compete for winery tours."

◍

They all checked out of the hotel. Leo said his goodbyes and was off to the train station and Martina took a cab to the airport. The hotel suggested that rentals there would have a better selection and cheaper prices than in town. Marcus moved to the hotel's computer room to wait for Martina and to dash a quick email off to New York. While sitting there, he overheard a conversation in the hotel reception area. With his moderate to poor understanding of Italian he was able to determine that someone had come in and was asking for him. He clearly heard the receptionist say in English quite loudly, "Mr. Peterson and the others checked out. I believe they were going to the airport. I know nothing other than that." And that was followed with a long comment in fast Italian that he couldn't understand at all.

After he heard the questioner leave, he started out to the reception desk to get an explanation. Before he got to the door, the receptionist pushed him back in and said, "I would suggest you stay here until Ms. Bufalino comes back. And then I would suggest you both leave immediately. I don't know where you're going, but I don't want to know. That individual that was questioning your whereabouts is definitely associated with the Mafia here in town. That I know."

◍

Jenna seldom got to the office before 7:30. Today, for some reason, the normal hustle and bustle of Manhattan was calm and the commute flawless. She was sitting down at her desk at 7:10. Starting her computer, she was surprised to see a notice that email was waiting.

Who would be emailing at this hour, she thought. Opening up the mail program, she saw it was from Marcus and a broad smile crossed her face. As she opened the email and began to read, her face went pale with fear.

Oh my God, the Mafia is going to kill him, flashed through her mind. But as she read further, where he described the plan they were about to execute, her face turned red and jealous rage erupted in her mind. *Marcus is mine. I developed our relationship and nobody is going to break it up.*

"That bitch Martina," she yelled out loud. "I know what she's up to and it's not gonna happen." Getting up and slamming the door, she marched to the department head's office.

Marcus could not believe what he saw as he came out of the hotel, pulling both his and Martina's luggage. There was Martina, parked in a bright blue Maserati Gran Torino convertible with the top down.

"Martina, how did you pull that off? I was only kidding about the sports car," said Marcus.

"Well, it's a long story, but the short of it is they were out of Fiat Pandas, which are the standard low price rentals. So he had to give me an upgrade. When I told him we would probably end up in Rome, he offered this car. It's six years old and he's been waiting for an opportunity to get it back to Rome. It's obviously a high-priced rental and the last user dropped it off here. Getting someone to rent it from here has been next to impossible. It has two bucket seats behind the driver so there's room for Leo. Marcus, you get your wish. A beautiful ride through the Tuscan vineyards to San Gimignano. Have you ever driven a sports car?"

"Martina, you wouldn't believe, that's one of my hobbies. I'm a member of the Monticello sports car club in New York. They have their own track, run several races, and conduct training programs. A couple of times a year there are events where you get to drive a variety of foreign sports cars provided by the dealers. I have driven a Maserati and a Lamborghini. I'm ready. Let's load up and go."

In less than 10 minutes they were out of Florence and on the open road, whipping along through vineyards and olive groves. "This drives like a dream," said Marcus. "Oh, I got so carried away with the car I forgot to relate what happened at the hotel before you got back from the airport."

Marcus then told Martina about the suspected Mafia inquiry. As he spoke and with his eyes on the road, he did not see Martina's facial expression change from relaxed to fear and then determination.

"There's a wide spot in the road coming up. Pull over for a second," Martina said. As they came to a stop, Martina slowly pulled her slacks up on her right leg and carefully removed the Beretta that was strapped there. Marcus looked on with surprise.

"Marcus, this is my spare." She said, "I suggest you begin to carry it. My primary firearm is a Walther PPK. That's in my shoulder holster." As she said this, she tapped her chest on the left side. "I assume you know how to use it and let's hope it's never necessary."

"I scored pretty well in my operational training. I wasn't aware you carried a firearm. Your bolero jacket hides it well."

"Most always on operational assignments. Of course, on our last operation we were on a cruise ship and all firearms are forbidden on board."

CHAPTER 3

San Gimignano

T he drive to San Gimignano was a total delight for Marcus. The Maserati handled well on the winding roads through the vineyards and olive groves. He took one side road after another, but with the GPS they were always able to keep their heading toward town. It was late afternoon when they approached the walled village.

"Wow, look at all those towers," said Marcus.

"It's said that in medieval times San Gimignano was a major stopping place on the main road from France to Rome. Recorded history says there were a total of 72 tower houses then but now there are only 14. If we get a chance while we are here, we may be able to explore one or two. I believe one or more house small museums," said Martina.

The drive into the town center and the Leon Bianco hotel was a little dicey through the narrow streets that in places were filled with wandering tourists. As they arrived in front of the hotel, Martina exited the car and a bellman appeared almost instantly. Marcus unloaded their two bags while the conversation ensued between Martina and the bellman in Italian. She turned to Marcus and handed him a card she received from the bellman and said, "All parking is in lots outside the wall. The hotel has a private guarded one where we have to put our car. It's just a short way away. Here is the address. You can put it in the GPS."

At about that time, a smartly dressed gentlemen exited the hotel, exchanged pleasantries with the bellman that was bringing in their bags, and walked directly to Marcus and Martina. His words, "*Per favore*, I'll be happy to show you the way. It will save me a walk to my car which is parked there."

Martina was totally caught off guard. The man's voice was familiar but somehow his appearance was not. She felt she should know him, but before she could say a word, the gentleman hoped into the car with Marcus and he drove off. The conversation between them was a rapid, "turn here, watch those children, careful, turn left at the next intersection, slow down, the next right will put you in the lot and welcome to San Gimignano, Agent Peterson. I am CIA Agent Nelson here on another operation. You can call me Brady."

The stranger was a rapid talker and the last words from him startled Marcus as he pulled into the lot. Agent Nelson continued with, "I just happen to be in the vicinity and when I got the email from Agent Adams, I thought it opportune to make contact. I expect to be in the area for the next few days so I will give you my cell number. Please make contact if you need any backup. Also, a word of caution. You are in Italy and here your primary mission is intelligence, not law enforcement. That should always be left to the local authorities. Assist only when requested."

"I understand," responded Marcus. "We experienced that situation yesterday in Florence."

Agent Nelson continued, "By the way, your makeover is impressive. Agent Adams enclosed pictures of both you and Agent Bufalino. I recognized her but I wouldn't have been able to recognize you at all. Oh, and I wouldn't mention to Martina Bufalino, the Interpol agent, who I am. It's best that I remain undercover and exposed only if absolutely necessary. However, it is good that you are teamed with her. She can best steer you clear of the Mafia."

"How is that?" asked Marcus as he pulled the Maserati into a parking place and began putting the top up.

"Italian Interpol agents appear to have their way. You will see," said Brady as he quickly exited the car and walked away.

Marcus didn't see him pull his phone out of his pocket as he was walking and before he could call out to him, his phone rang. Answering, he heard, "Now you have my number. Be careful, but enjoy. *Ciao*."

Martina met Marcus in front of the hotel when he had walked back from the parking lot and much to his surprise, she said, "I've settled us in our rooms. Let's walk to the square and find a place to eat, and who was that gentleman who directed you to the parking lot?"

"He never mentioned his name, and when we arrived at the lot, he hopped out of the car and was gone," lied Marcus.

"Somehow he seemed very familiar to me. Like I really knew him but didn't. Oh well, not to worry. Let's go eat."

Which they did in spades. Not only did they find a place to eat, but they stopped in several nightspots for a drink where Martina questioned bartenders about workers in the different wineries. With the drive during the day and the evening's adventure, Marcus was totally fatigued as Martina led him to their room in the hotel. Entering, he spotted the layout: one large king-sized bed. His thought, *I almost could have predicted this but I'm so tired I'll never be able to take advantage of it.*

Martina then startled him by firmly saying, "I don't know how you played it with Jenna on your last operation. But as far as the bathroom is concerned, I'm first at night and second in the morning." It was almost like a command and she then quickly went there, her thoughts being,

You may have feelings for your last partner, but you are about to forget all about her. When this mission is over, you may be taking me to the US.

Martina carefully prepared for the big seduction. Shower, loose hair, slight amount of makeup, hint of perfume, no nightgown but a sheer robe. She was ready. Exiting the bathroom, her anticipated passionate plunge was shattered. The bedspread on the king-sized bed was pulled down exposing two made-up twin beds pushed together with a fully clothed Marcus passed out on one.

⑩

It was ten o'clock when Marcus woke up fully clothed. The bed next to him was made up and there was no sign of Martina. His cell phone was dead, not having been charged. He had not much of a memory of last night and a pounding headache. *Maybe a shower and clean clothes will bring me back to life,* he thought, *Where could she have gone?*

Getting up, he spotted the glass of water, two aspirin and a note on the dressing table which he read out loud. "You had a wonderful night. Barhopping seemed to agree with you, that is, until you passed out. The aspirin should help but I'll call you later in the morning to see if you survived. Love, Martina."

I guess I sort of blew it last night, he thought as he got up, plugged in the cell phone, and staggered to the shower.

⑩

Exiting the shower, Marcus thought he heard the suite door close. Remembering when he checked in the strange sound it made when it was closed, he had mentioned to Martina that no one would ever be able to sneak into the room regardless of how they unlocked the door. Hearing this sound he called out,

"Martina, is that you?" and slipping on the robe hanging on the back of the door, he opened it to enter.

To his surprise a complete stranger was there mumbling something in Italian and coming straight at him with a knife in hand. Marcus's martial arts training quickly kicked in and he delivered a fast thrust to the assailant's throat as he approached. The surprised assailant dropped the knife and grabbed for his throat, falling to the floor gasping for air. The crushed trachea caused a horrible death. Between the lack of air due to the wind pipe collapsing and the blood, it was almost a minute or more before the assailant choked to death.

It was then that the now fully-charged cell phone on the bedside table rang. Picking it up, Marcus could see it was from Martina and he said in a somewhat nervous voice, "Martina. I think we have a small problem. I believe I just killed someone."

"Marcus, calm yourself. Tell me what happened," said Martina.

Marcus took a couple of deep breaths and in a calmer voice explained to Martina everything that had just happened. The phone was dead for a few seconds. Then in a firm voice, Martina responded, "Marcus, get dressed immediately and leave the suite. Go into the square and go to the gelateria there. Get a table in the back and stay there until I either come or call you." Then in a louder voice, "Do it now," and the phone went dead.

Marcus, dressed in a Nike sweat shirt and pants, sat in the Gelateria Dondoli where Martina had told him to go. While waiting, he passed the time devouring a huge bowl of gelato. *I wonder how she's handling things,* he thought. *What will she tell the authorities and the hotel, and what will happen with the body?* It was then he remembered Brady's last words to him. "Interpol agents have their way."

His thoughts were immediately answered as Martina walked in and sitting at the table said,

"I think you are still okay."

Surprised by that opening, Marcus responded, "What do you mean, okay?"

"I believe that Mafia thug followed me to see who I was with. Discovering it was with you when you spoke English, he immediately decided you should die as ordered. He obviously didn't have time to tell anyone that the dark-haired man with me was really Marcus Peterson before you killed him. Oh, the body has been taken care of. You probably saved the Italian government money as he was a wanted hit man of the Mafia. He definitely wasn't a local. They found his red

Vespa parked behind the hotel in an alley." Then looking at what Marcus had in front of him, Martina asked, "Gelato for breakfast?"

◉

Despite the severe crosswind, the Gulfstream G650 made a perfect landing on the privately-owned airfield outside of Palermo. It taxied back to the two waiting black limos at the end of the field. Colombian drug lords rarely leave their native country with the exception of one, the daring and most-wanted and most powerful, Carlos Calisto. His private jet avails his entry into countries totally unannounced, bypassing any immigration. His drug-smuggling operation to Europe and the US is infamous as his delivery mode is ever changing, frustrating the local authorities. This meeting with his local Mafia contact was critical to the expansion he had in mind.

As Carlos, dressed in a Palm Beach suit and sporting a Panama hat, exited his plane, a single portly individual in a dark suit exited the leading limo. They met and shook hands. "Welcome back to Sicily, Carlos. It has been a while since your last visit. Our operation in the north is going well; you should be happy. Now what brings you here?" said Luciano Guerra, Sicilian Mafia Don.

"I'm happy to return and yes, I am pleased, my Mafia friend. We are both doing well. I'm here to view the operation and explore its possible expansion. Smuggling across the US southern border is becoming extremely difficult. Expansion of this operation to other cities in the US would be my goal."

"I am sure you will be welcomed at the winery. Come, we have a chopper waiting at another field. It will take us up to the winery in a short time," said Luciano as he ushered Carlos to the waiting limos.

◉

Marcus and Martina spent the afternoon and now early evening touring the local bars and eating places in town. They would enter an establishment, picking a table in a crowded area, and order something to eat or drink. Martina would be listening to the conversation around.

Marcus was never to speak to avoid being discovered as an American. As they sat at a table either drinking or munching on what they had ordered Martina would occasionally speak to Marcus in Italian and he would nod in agreement and occasionally respond with a "*Si.*"

The current establishment they were in appeared to be one of the local watering holes and began filling up with what appeared to be locals as opposed to tourists, possibly workers stopping for a drink on the way home. Fairly loud conversation echoed in the room. Sipping his glass of wine, Marcus noticed an intent look appear on Martina's face.

She must be hearing something interesting, he thought and then out of the blue she reached across the table, grabbing his hand and speaking in perfect Swedish, saying, "The four men at the table next to us all work at the Tenuta Toscano winery. They are discussing their workday at the winery and it's very interesting."

Marcus, totally caught off guard, was speechless for a moment. He hadn't heard Swedish since he was a small boy. He remembered visiting his grandparents, where Swedish was spoken all the time and during his early years he picked up enough of the language to converse with his grandparents. In later years, however, English was spoken all the time at family gatherings. His Swedish language capabilities thus diminished. Hearing Swedish from Martina was a total shock. His brain went into high gear. *How did she know I was Swedish? Where did she learn Swedish? What did she just say? I have got to respond and not in English. Oh, shit.*

Pulling words out of his memory, in broken Swedish he responded, "I think you said something about the table next to us and the winery we're trying to get to. If you speak a little slower, I may better understand some of what you say."

She responded in Swedish, "I will fill you in when we leave. Look affectionate and hold my hand. My eyes are on you, but my ears are on the table next to us."

"I understand," responded Marcus, holding both of Martina's hands across the table. He looked lovingly into her eyes. Anyone watching this couple from afar would probably assume they were just two young people madly in love.

As Martina continued listening to the conversation at the table next to them, Marcus's brain switched gears. Ignoring the sounds around him, he began to really study Martina. *She is really quite attractive*, he thought. *That white peasant-girl blouse leaves little to the imagination. Damn, what have I been missing.*

Leo was a little discouraged. Livorno didn't turn out quite as Martina had described. Oh, Sophia was nice and attractive as Martina said she was, but she was all business. In fact, when he arrived at the tour agency she was nowhere to be found. They met the next morning at breakfast. Most of the day was spent going over the details of the bus tour. It was interesting. She had considerable facts about the winery as well as San Gimignano that he was unaware of. But by midafternoon, it was getting quite boring. "Sofia, enough of this. Is there anything in Livorno to do? Sites to see? Places to eat? Nightclubs? I think I'm prepared enough for the bus trip. Show me your town," said Leo with a questioning look on his face. "Where do the cruise ships dock? Is there a cruise terminal?"

"There is a cruise terminal but it is not used by the large cruise ships. They all come into the large container-ship docks. Passengers are not allowed to walk from their ships into town. Taxis and buses, including ours, will go out and be parked on the wharf right next to the arriving vessel. So, to view that area you'll have to wait till tomorrow when we go out on our bus.

"Now, about my town. I thought you'd never ask. Come, we are off to Alcatraz for an early dinner," said Sophia as she grabbed Leo's hand and they headed to the door. "It's a five-star restaurant. I hope you have your credit card. While there, I will tell you about the sites in town. Depending on the time, we may be able to hit one. The evening, however, will be at Bimbo's, my favorite nightclub."

The Agusta helicopter safely settled down in the circle outlined on the great lawn in front of the chateau at Tenuta Toscano. Giovanni Toscano waved at the chopper and walked toward it as it powered down. Helping the occupants deplane, he said, "Carlos, Luciano, welcome back to my humble home. I was happily surprised when I got the call saying you were coming. Come, I have a feast prepared for you. We have much to discuss."

A generous epicurean dinner table was set in one of their wine cellars, well out of earshot of many and amid the stacked oak barrels aging their wine. The three were served appetizers of Tuscan cheeses and bruschetta followed by a course of ravioli and ricotta spinach, then a second course of wild boar prepared with olives. With this, copious quantities of wine were poured. Light conversation in English ensued.

"Giovanni, your humble poor coca plant grower from Colombia finds this feast outstanding," said Carlos.

"You honor a poor winemaker with your presence," responded Giovanni.

"Gentlemen, enough of the niceties. We have issues to discuss," said Luciano. "First, Carlos, explain to us the black cocaine method of shipment that you have implemented. Will it complicate our infusion process? I hope you can explain the process for cleaning the cocaine before it's infused into the wine. And Giovanni, you must inform us of what you've learned from your cousin who works in the anti-Mafia investigation department."

"You have Mafia family in the government?" questioned Carlos. "That's similar to how we operate in Colombia."

"Yes, I will review with your people the process we use in Colombia to remove the additive that we use on the cocaine coloring it black."

Marcus was overwhelmed with Martina's conversation as they exited the last restaurant and walked to the hotel. She started talking like a news broadcaster. This went on as they went to their suite only pausing as they sauntered through the hotel hall. "Remember that last restaurant we were at. The man sitting opposite the blonde with the fuzzy hair and a mustache, well, he said that his workday today involved . . ."

She went on and on, talking a mile a minute as she went to the bathroom to get ready for bed.

Very little that she said registered with Marcus. Having listened to Italian that he couldn't understand much of all the afternoon and evening, he had begun to just turn conversation off. Instead, he concentrated on Martina's physical attributes. The entire time was spent sitting across from her at different restaurants staring at her and nodding occasionally. Thus, he began to conjure up interesting thoughts about the attractive woman he was facing. *I like the way her eyes twinkle when she smiles, that dimple on the left cheek. She has a beautiful neck. Her blouse shows just enough of her breasts to present a very sexual appearance. An encounter with her in bed might be quite wonderful,* he had thought then and continued to think now.

She exited the bathroom in the thin negligee she had worn the night before and lay on the bed but continued to rattle on about who they had seen and what they had said. Marcus decided it was time to make his move. He lay down beside her, stopping her chatter with a passionate kiss and whispering in her ear, "please be quiet." He began to lightly brush his fingers along her arm, her cheek, her neck and downward along the curve of her waist and her hips, then slipped his hand inside her negligee. She turned to him and helped him undress. He continued to gently caress her, brushing his hand along the skin below her navel and then stroking back up around the curves of her breasts and along her ribs. She turned and responded by pulling his head to her chest. They made love over and over again, communicating with each other the entire time by only their eyes and touch.

Thoughts crossed Martina's mind. *This is what I had hoped for last night. I think I'm on my way to winning him over. A home in the US?*

CHAPTER 4

A Tuscany Morning

Martina never stirred when Marcus got up, donned his sweats and went out for his run. Sex with her last night was wonderful but left him a little perplexed as he still had strong feelings for Jenna back in New York. *The run should clear my head*, he thought. It was a beautiful clear morning with a slight breeze. The sun was just creeping up over the horizon. Outside the walls of San Gimignano he found a trail leading into an adjacent olive grove. At this time in the morning the only sign of life he encountered was a rabbit that crossed his path as he entered the grove. The run through the trees provided a welcoming change from the cobblestones of the town.

Exiting the grove, he found himself on the same road that they had entered the city on two days ago. *The run back to the hotel should be easy. I won't have to use the GPS on my phone,* he thought. And he was right. As he passed the hotel parking lot, he was happy to see that the Maserati was still parked where he had left it a day and a half ago. The run through the streets of San Gimignano was also a pleasure as they were totally deserted. Arriving at the hotel, he was pleased to see Martina sitting alone at a table outside. That meant he could speak English. The table was set with what appeared to be a large pot of coffee, a pot of warm milk and a huge basket of *fette biscottate* and *cornetti* (croissants). He hoped that there would also be a side of apricot marmalade.

"Martina, you finally woke up. You were sound asleep when I left this morning," he said as he came up to the table and sat. "Breakfast looks great and my run generated a pretty good appetite. By the way, it's time to talk. You have to tell me all that you heard yesterday. Will it affect how we operate on the bus trip today?"

"Yes, it might. Let me explain," she said, but her thoughts were, *What about last night. Was that just a dream? He is all businesses this morning. It's as if it never happened. We made love and I felt he was really attracted to me. What happened? Oh well, on to the business at hand.*

"The hypothesis we have about the winery appears to be true, but how we verify it by going on this wine tasting excursion could be a problem. It seems there is a separate building called the infusion laboratory and it may be attached to the bottling process facility. That isn't clear. Remember that last restaurant we were in and the table of three workers that was next to us and I was listening so intently to? Well, one of the workers sitting at the table evidently had just been reassigned to that facility. He was the young blonde man and he was describing to the others his new job. He spoke of black powder arriving at the facility in fertilizer bags. After processing, removing the dye and whatever else was added, it became a white slurry that was then infused into the wine before it was bottled. He went on to say he thought he was working in some sort of chemical plant instead of a winery.

"I have heard of additives being added to cocaine to change its color and to inhibit its discovery by dogs that are used to sniff for drugs. This supposedly helps getting it past import inspections. That could be what's going on here," said Martina.

"Well, I'm sure our planned wine-tasting excursion will not take us anywhere near that facility. We better call Leo. I'm beginning to doubt that our original game plan is going to provide us anything positive."

"On the contrary, yes, we will call Leo, but the excursion is still a good plan. It should at least give us a little knowledge of the lay of the land at the winery. While out there we might discover some alternate ways to locate the so-called infusion building. If it's typical of the other large wineries in Italy, they probably offer other activities to get you out there. Remember, the primary goal of any winery is to promote and sell their wine. Getting people to visit their vineyard and winery is paramount in accomplishing that."

⊕

Leo's head was still spinning as he went down to breakfast. *That Sophia is alright,* he thought. *I had a fabulous time at the club Bimbo's. She's a terrific dancer, no matter what I did she followed along. It would really be great to get to know her better. I sure hope our paths cross again sometime.*

"Oh, Sophia, there you are. Good morning," he said as he spotted Sophia in the facility's cafeteria. "Let me get some breakfast; I will be right with you," he said as he rushed over to the buffet line.

Setting down his tray and sitting at Sophia's table, he continued, "I just wanted to tell you I had a great time last night. Livorno is not too bad a town. By the way, when do we have to be on the excursion bus? Do we get out on the wharf before the ship comes in? I'm sort of excited about this. I've never been close to or on a cruise ship or a container ship. I guess I've just never been in a busy port."

"Thank you. I had a great time too. Bimbo's is my favorite night-club. Now about today. I called my contact on board the Golden Duchess this morning and she said they expected to arrive at seven. Between the time it takes to dock and clear immigration, passenger debarking will probably be close to nine o'clock. That's when the buses should be there so that means we probably will be leaving here at about 8:30. It's only seven now, so enjoy your breakfast. We have plenty of time," Sophia replied.

Their conversation was rudely interrupted by the loud ringing of Leo's cell phone. "I'm sorry," he said, "I use this also as my alarm clock. I forgot to turn down the ring volume after getting up this morning. I better get this call."

"Martina, hello. Good morning, what's up? Are you ready for the excursion?"

"Let me check."

Looking at Sophia, he said, "She wants to know if the excursion is scheduled to go to San Gimignano before the winery, as we had hoped."

"Tell her yes, and we should be arriving at the tour bus parking area sometime between 10 and 10:30. Tell her I look forward to seeing her again."

After doing that, Leo's face became quite serious as he listened intently on the phone. Several minutes later he said, "I'll tell her. She might be able to help us. See you soon. *Ciao*."

⦿

Snaking their way out to the Darsena Toscana cruise ship pier, their bus passed several container ship wharfs in the commercial port area. Containers stacked high on ships and on piers both were being loaded and unloaded. There were already several buses queued up in front of the ship as well as several taxis when they arrived. The nineteen-deck Golden Duchess loomed high above the scene.

"Sophia, are we late? Look at all those buses that are here before us. And the ship, it's huge. I had no idea." said Leo.

"Not to worry. We are not late. They schedule us in so that the buses are lined up according to where they are off to. We are not the only tour company in Livorno; at least two others besides ours will be servicing the ship today. The ship carries over 2000 passengers and many of them will be going on tours as far away as Florence and as close as Pisa.

"You might not have noticed when you boarded, but the driver has a Duchess sign in the windshield with a big blue number five on it. Our particular tour is listed as Duchess blue five. And you will see when the passengers board our bus, they will all be wearing blue Duchess number five stickers on their coat or shirt. The cruise line does an outstanding job of organizing the shore excursions. You will see, they will be debarking the passengers by tour group and each group will have a Duchess crew member with them. His or her responsibility is to keep the group together and make sure they get back to the ship before sailing and to make sure we do a decent job.

Our contracts depend on the feedback the cruise line gets from them as well as the passengers."

The whole area looked a little like organized chaos. Passengers were pouring off the ship and lining up in groups in front of different crew members who held up signs with tour numbers. When the group was fully assembled, the crew member would lead them off to their proper bus. And as the buses loaded, they would immediately pull out.

As their bus pulled in and parked, Sophia said, "Leo, you stay here in our seats. These front seats are reserved for us. I'll be out front collecting a ticket from each passenger before they board the bus. When we're all loaded, I will come back on board and sit with you. The assigned crew member will come on board last and probably sit in the back."

As the passengers were loading the bus, the attractive young blonde crewmember standing next to Sophia caught Leo's eye. *Wow,* he thought. *She looks pretty hot. Maybe I ought to take up cruising.*

The last passenger of the group got on board and almost immediately a senior Duchess crew member arrived speaking to Sophia and the assigned group crewmember, then waving them off. They both boarded the bus with the assigned crew member going to the back, and Sophia still standing. She grabbed the mic to start her welcoming speech. Then she momentarily put her hand over it and bent down, saying to Leo, "I saw you eyeing our assigned crew member. She's a nice gal, name is Jenna. I'll introduce you to her after we get rolling." Then standing up, she started with, "Welcome to Livorno, welcome to Tuscany, welcome to Italy. My name is Sophia and I will be your guide today."

It was 9:30 when Martina and Marcus got to the tour bus parking lot outside the walls of San Gimignano. Some buses had already arrived, but none from the Golden Duchess.

"Are we too early?" said Marcus.

"No, I think we are about right," said Martina. "Leo's phone call this morning indicated they expected to be here between 10 and 10:30.

He said we have to watch for a bus with a number five in the front window. He also said when it arrives we should wait until Sophia leads the group tour off the bus and starts walking into the city. He will stay behind and get off at the end."

The buses were coming in at 10 to 15 minute intervals. "I guess this wouldn't be the day to drive in from Livorno. That two-lane road with all these buses would make for a horrible drive," said Marcus.

"Yes and no," said Martina. "They can be coming from both directions. Tour groups from the ships will be coming from Livorno while land tours could be coming from Florence."

It was an interesting sight. As each bus pulled in, the front door would open and out would pop a tour guide holding some sort of standard: a flag, an umbrella, or a sign. His or her group would follow like sheep as they were led off into the city.

"Contrary to what Leo said on the phone, I want to meet the bus and give Sophia a hug when she gets off. I haven't seen her in quite a while," said Martina. "Oh look, here comes a bus with a number five in window. That's got to be it. Come, let's meet it."

They rushed over to the slot the bus pulled into and were in greeting position as it came to a halt. The doors opened and Sophia stepped out, holding up a sign with a large blue number five on it. Before she could turn to help the passengers off, Martina grabbed her in a bear hug and said, "Welcome to San Gimignano. It's great to see you again."

"And you also," said Sophia. "By the way, our assigned Duchess crew member says she knows you. She is in the back of the bus so will be getting off last, along with Leo."

"That's probably possible. I worked with a lot of the shore excursion crew members when I was on board the Golden Duchess under cover."

"Got to lead the group in. We can meet at the fountain when I turn them loose on their own. Then we can catch up. Stay here. As I said, Leo and Jenna will be off last." And with that said, Sophia turned and trotted off toward with the gates of the city with the group members following her as they discharged from the bus.

Jenna? That bitch. How the hell did she get over here, thought Martina. *She could ruin everything and possibly blow this operation and get Marcus killed.*

"Martina, did she say Jenna is on board? How could that be? She's supposed to be my contact in New York. I had a Skype call with her four days ago," said Marcus. "I wonder if she will recognize me."

As the last passenger got off the bus, Jenna came to the door with Leo close behind. Before descending the steps she looked towards Marcus and Martina with a puzzled expression on her face and called out, "Martina, where is Marcus?"

Well, that is a plus. She didn't recognize Marcus. Our transformation of him worked, thought Martina.

Her thoughts were immediately shattered as Marcus waved his hand and called out, "Jenna, I'm here. It's me. You look great in that Duchess uniform. How did you get over here? We just spoke a few days ago. You're supposed to be in New York."

Hearing those words, Jenna leaped off the bus into Marcus's arms, giving him a very passionate kiss. Under her breath, Martina said, "Oh, shit," then loudly added, "Quick, back on the bus, all of you. We have to talk."

⬤⬤

The square in San Gimignano filled with visitors and conspicuous was the huge queue in front of the Gelateria Dondoli. Many of Sophia's group were in that queue. After turning them loose, she had positioned herself on the fountain stairs set in the square center.

Martina came up. They hugged, sat down, and began a conversation in French, assuming that any locals overhearing the conversation wouldn't understand it.

"Where are the others?" asked Sophia.

"They are back on the bus. Leo and Marcus are explaining to Jenna our overall plan, the situation with Marcus, his disguise, and the fact that we are pretending to be an Italian couple on vacation. Needless to say, I don't think she will be so happy with the latter. I believe she and Marcus developed a relationship on their last assignment. Oh well, possibly her loss, my gain. Leo also will be getting his bag that was stowed in the bus's baggage section and transferring it to our hotel. Marcus will be repositioning our car out to the intersection of the main road and the road into San Gimignano with the intent of getting back to the bus before your passenger group returns. I believe you told them that they had to be back on board by 11:45. That left less than an hour to accomplish all of that.

"But enough about them. Let me explain the plan for the winery. As you recall, the buses are usually met by winery personnel in the parking lot in close proximity to the building where the wine tastings are usually conducted. Marcus and I will get off the bus last. We will explain to one of the greeters that as opposed to ship passengers in the group, we are staying in San Gimignano and joined the tour there. Further, that we would be interested in any day tours that may be available and could we be taken to the office where that could be arranged. With luck, they'll accommodate us and after arranging something for tomorrow, we will come back and join the wine tasting. When the tasting is over, we will leave on the bus with you. Then you can drop us off at the San Gimignano turnoff on your way back to Livorno. On a day tour of the vineyard and winery, we might have a better chance of locating the so-called infusion facility," said Martina.

"Sounds like a great plan. Let's get back in the gelato line before we have to be back on the bus," responded Sophia as she got up and led Martina over to the gelateria. "Oh, look over there. Isn't that Leo wheeling a bag into the Leon Bianco hotel across the way?"

"Yes, that's where we are staying," responded Martina.

The cool breeze and the shade of the olive tree sent a little chill through Jenna as she sat on the huge Golden Duchess blanket that was spread on the ground. She gazed over at Marcus as she buttoned her blouse and finished dressing. Her mind was spinning with thoughts. *That was so wonderful. I really do miss him. After that frolic, I'm sure he still loves me. Oh, you are now totally engrossed in assembling that mini drone I brought over, but I know you won't forget making love just a short*

while ago. It was then she saw a little crimson dot dancing on his chest and called out, "Marcus, No!" as the shot rang out.

"Jenna, Jenna, wake up," said Leo, shaking her.

"Oh, Oh, I'm sorry. Is he alright?" she said.

"Who"? asked Leo "You were sound asleep"

"Oh, I must have been dreaming. I saw Marcus get shot. I'm sorry. When you and Marcus left, I lay down on the back seat to close my eyes for a minute. I haven't really had much sleep since I left New York. I caught the red eye flight to Marseille to get on the Golden Duchess and it's been a whirlwind of activity since. Where is Marcus? I have a package for him."

"He should be along in a minute and the passengers should also start to arrive back on the bus. We will be leaving as soon as they all get back along with Sophia and Martina. Sophia wants to leave by noon."

CHAPTER 5

The Toscano Vineyard

O nce on the property of the Tenuta Toscano, the tour bus wound its way through the vast vineyards, an olive grove and finally a large oak grove bordering again another vineyard. The parking lot was a short walk to their wine-tasting facility housing several tasting rooms. There were two small intimate rooms set among wine barrels and racks of wine bottles and a large tasting room in a glassed-in veranda overlooking the vineyard. Here the tour was seated at two long tables accommodating 10 on each side. They were set with two wine glasses and a small plate at each place and bottles of water in the center. Jenna, Leo, and Sophia seated themselves at the end of one table. They had reserved two seats at the other end for Marcus and Martina.

The hostess standing at the head of both tables announced, "Welcome, everybody, to the Toscano Winery, a family-owned vineyard. I am NatalieToscano, great-granddaughter of the founder. Today we will be tasting eight wines paired with special dishes, one of which will be my grandmother's famous lasagna. The recipe is a family secret. It's topped with truffle oil made here from truffles gathered under that oak grove you passed through on your way here. This will be paired with our special reserve Chianti Classico Riserva."

A young man arrived at the tables and began pouring a white wine. "We will start with Vernaccia di San Gimignano," continued Natalie. "It will be paired with Tuscan cheese and bruschetta."

Leo leaned over toward Jenna and Sophia with a slight grin on his face saying, "Oh, the ordeals one must endure when on assignment."

◍

Martina and Marcus were able to arrange a vineyard tour for the following day and walking back to the wine tasting, Martina suddenly paused, saying, "Oh, shit. Don't stare, Marcus, but coming towards us on that path from the large chateau appears to be Carlos Calisto and Luciano Guerra. I don't have any idea who the third one is."

"What would Carlos be doing over here in Italy? I thought drug lords never left Colombia," said Marcus.

"I have no idea and hopefully, they may not recognize us. You are in your Italian disguise and I am not in a Duchess Cruise Line uniform or wearing my hair the way I did on the Golden Duchess. If they are going to the wine tasting, they sure as hell will recognize Jenna. What can we do?"

"I say we play it cool and hope for the best. I'm sure if Guerra recognizes Jenna and speaks to her, she will be clever in her response. Walk a little faster. We should be able to beat them there and warn Jenna. If Calisto and Guerra are here, I think we can pretty much be sure this is the source of the cocaine wine and our only chore will be to gain some form of visual evidence without being discovered or killed."

"What a pleasant thought. Oh shit, Guerra and Calisto are coming our way. The other guy is going toward the tasting room."

"Quick, cut across the lawn. We're a little late for the tasting and our hurry would be expected."

◍

Walking from the chateau, the three men paused.

"Luciano, you can take Carlos down to the infusion facility. Just cut through the parking lot over where the tour bus is. You will recognize the path," said Giovanni. "I have to make an appearance at the wine tasting. This group is from the cruise ship and they are always prospective wine buyers, not only here, but when they return to their homes. I try to make them feel special and assure them that they will always receive the discounts that will be offered today at their visit. I usually follow up with an email to those that buy while they are here. You would be surprised at the number of sales that generates."

"That's a nice approach. Maybe I should apply that marketing to my cocaine in the states," said Carlos with a slight smile.

"Now that would be a different approach to the drug market," continued Giovanni, also smiling. "By the way, the cut I get for the wine infusion is fine but I still need the vineyard to make a profit. Those books can be monitored by the government." Giovanni split off and headed to the wine tasting while Carlos and Luciano headed towards the infusion facility.

"Carlos, about the black cocaine?" said Luciano.

"Yes, that's the way I am shipping it and they are receiving it. When you get down to the infusion facility you may see stacks of what appear to be fertilizer bags out in front of the facility. They should have arrived on a container ship yesterday."

"Yes, Giovani mentioned it to me when I called to tell him we were coming. He also mentioned that the shipment sailed right through customs at the port. Drug dogs picked up no scent and the bags marked as fertilizer attracted little attention. Great move. He didn't say anything about black cocaine. Now I understand. That should keep the authorities off our back for a while. He obviously is having trouble removing it from the cocaine."

"Yes, I'll explain it to his people. It's a simple process," responded Carlos.

◉

As the wine tasting proceeded, after each serving the conversation around the two tables seemed to rise an octave or two. The last wine to be tasted was Vin Beato, a dessert wine that was paired with Italian almond cookies. The guests appeared delighted and the conversation around the tables grew louder.

Natalie had to almost shout to get their attention. "Ladies and gentlemen, please!" And as they quieted down, she continued, "I hope you have enjoyed the tasting and now may I provide you the grand finale. I am pleased to be able to offer the wines you have tasted today at a 30% discount. You may use the order forms placed in front of you. I can assure you that wines ordered today will appear on your doorstep within three weeks. Please, I will be at the desk in the back of the room to accept all orders. Either cash or credit card is acceptable. Thank you."

Short applause followed and everyone stood up from the tables and milled around, some following Natalie to the desk at the back of the room. Jenna grabbed Marcus's arm, ushering him out to the surrounding garden saying, "Please come with me. We have Bureau business to discuss." Marcus, a little surprised, dutifully followed her out the door.

Leo and Sophia walked over to Martina, Leo saying, "Martina, it looks like your faux husband has been kidnapped."

Martina responded with a Cheshire cat grin, "Oh, not to worry. She is just trying to rekindle a shipboard romance that I feel has pretty much cooled."

"You sound pretty confident." commented Sophia.

With a smug expression Martina responded, "You must understand. When it comes to *amore*, we Italians are the professionals."

"Marcus, I'm still taken by you," said Jenna, giving him a passionate kiss. Then breaking away and taking a cell phone out of her purse, she continued, "and the Bureau is a concerned about your welfare. Please, give me your phone. This is your new phone. We are not sure about the capabilities of the Mafia over here but we have disabled the GPS function of this phone. If they have the wherewithal, they will not be able to track you. Further, if they are tracking you, they will believe you are returning to the ship and sailing away, as I will be carrying your old phone."

"I hadn't thought about that, but from our conversations with the authorities over here, I'm sure the Mafia is high tech. Thanks so much. Oh, what's in the bag you brought me?"

"It's one of our new toys at the Bureau. When you described your game plan to me, I thought it would be ideal. It's called a Baby Elfie. It's a mini foldable drone with dual remote control. It's not much bigger than the size of your hand and can be carried in a little case that also holds its remote controller and can strap to your arm. Its battery gives it a flight time of about seven minutes and a distance capability of about 700 meters. You'll be able to take still or motion pictures using your phone. The new phone I gave you has the app installed. I suggest you fly the drone with its remote and have Martina or Leo use the phone to take pictures during its flight. I would practice in an open field or parking lot to get the hang of it."

Before Marcus could say anything, Jenna was back in his arms with another passionate kiss. Then breaking away, she said, "We must get back to the group as they will be going back to the bus. Have fun with your new toy and don't forget me. I love you." Marcus grabbed her in a bear hug, then hand in hand they walked back to the tasting room.

As the tour bus approached the intersection where their Maserati was parked, Marcus, who was sitting in the back with Jenna, gave her a goodbye kiss and made his way forward. Approaching Sophia, Martina, and Leo, who were seated up front, he said, "Martina, as a preventive measure, I suggest you and Leo get off where I parked the car. I will get off a little further down the road and walk back. If anyone is watching the car and planning an unscrupulous greeting, I will be the backup. The car is parked at the edge of an olive grove with considerable ground foliage along the road. I should be able to get back unnoticed."

"Good thought, Marcus," said Martina. "We are both armed so we should be able to mitigate any villainous activity that we may encounter. I would be surprised if anything was planned on a main thoroughfare, but an ounce of precaution is worth a pound of valor."

⚏

Crossing the parking lot, Carlos and Luciano entered a small path in the adjacent oak grove.

"Carlos, the facility is on the other side of this oak grove. The ground slopes here and it's slightly downhill to the facility. By the way, the winery holds truffle hunts in season under these trees. The soil appears to be perfect for truffles. They have dogs that are trained to sniff them out," said Luciano.

"How do they keep the facility under wraps with public tours, etc," asked Carlos.

"Generally, people never go as far as the other side of the grove where the facility is. If they see the building in the distance and ask about it, they are told it's their bottling facility, which it is. It's a rather large building and one end is the bottling facility and the other, the laboratory where infusion takes place."

"Is the Toscano winery a part of your organization?" asked Carlos.

"Yes and no. Let's just say the Toscano winery has an un-dissolvable relationship with the Mafiosi," responded Luciano.

Carlos paused for a minute. Appearing a little fatigued due to the walk and facing Luciano, he said, "I understand. I have similar relationships in Colombia."

After the brief pause, they started walking again and Carlos continued his questioning, "The US operation, the Gambioni crime syndicate, how is that working? I see funds transferred electronically both to you and to me, but I have no direct contacts with the family in the US. In fact, my last contacts were in the Caribbean on that cruise ship where I convinced him to do business with us, as opposed to the Londono cartel."

"I am not surprised. Franco Gambioni, who you convinced to do business with us, was incarcerated when the cruise returned to New York.

running the family while his consigliere is working on getting him released."

"Well, that doesn't surprise me. Though she was an extremely attractive young lady, she was one tough cookie. Proficient in martial arts. She killed one of my men in San Juan when they tried to kidnap her."

"I wouldn't know about that, but she appears to be proficient and clever. The syndicate has gone into operating wine shops in the New York area, obviously to cover the cocaine operation. Where their diffusion laboratory is and its operation, I have no knowledge."

As they emerged from the oak grove they approached a set of stairs that descended to the entrance of the bottling facility. Before descending the steps, Luciano turned again to Carlos and said, "Oh, one other thing. When the Gambioni syndicate found out that the young CIA agent that spied on them during the Caribbean cruise was in Italy on assignment, they put a mark out on him suggesting his demise would be appreciated. To my knowledge no action has been taken on that. The family up here lost track of him after he entered Italy through Venice. They thought they had him in Florence, but they lost him after that."

"I'm not aware of how you operate your cartels in Colombia, but Mafia hit requests are usually accommodated as long as they don't involve interfamily squabbles. I can almost guarantee if he gets detected, he will experience a fatal accident."

As Marcus worked his way through the underbrush toward the area where he had parked the car, he had a premonition this could be his baptism under fire. His mind went into overdrive, reviewing the combat techniques he had learned at Camp Perry, commonly known in the CIA as "the farm." With the Beretta that Martina had given him drawn, he approached the clearing where the Maserati was parked. As he got closer, he heard Italian being spoken. One voice was clearly Martina's but the other sounded harsh and not familiar at all.

Entering the clearing as quietly as possible, he saw Martina and Leo standing next to the Maserati. They were facing a man whose back was towards him. The assailant stood at a slight angle such that Marcus could clearly see he was holding a gun. He also recognized that Martina was looking past the assailant and directly at him, slightly shaking her head up and down. Assuming that to be a sign, Marcus spoke out loudly, saying, "I wouldn't do that." The startled assailant turned towards Marcus and in that instant, Martina drew her Walther PPK and fired two shots into his chest and one into his head. His gun dropped from his hand as he fell forward, blood gushing from his wounds.

"Martina, what have you done?" cried Marcus.

In a quiet serious tone, Marina responded, "You obviously didn't understand the conversation that was going on when you arrived. Our assailant was asking us which one would like to die first. This was to be his vendetta. It appears the assailant you killed in the hotel was his brother. He also is a hit man for the Mafia."

"What do we do now? The body and all," asked Leo.

"Come get in the car, we must all leave immediately. I will make a call," said Martina.

Immediately Brady's last words to Marcus flashed in his mind, "Interpol agents have their way."

CHAPTER 6

Baby Elfie

C arlos and Luciano were just about to enter the bottling and infusion facility when Giovanni drove up in a golf cart. "Oh, I'm glad I caught you before you entered. Come, we will go around back. I want to show you our logistics operation," said Giovanni as he motioned them to join him in the golf cart.

"You picked a good day to visit. We are both shipping and receiving. The container ship arrived earlier this week from South America and, when loaded later this week, will be sailing directly to the United States. It's a bit unusual, but this time we received a container and will be placing a container on board the same ship."

As the golf cart pulled around the huge building, it entered a large parking area where the activity was taking place. A forklift was loading cases of wine in one container, while another forklift was removing skids of what appeared to be fertilizer bags from the other container.

"Ah, my fertilizer," said Carlos. "How do you like my packaging?" The fertilizer bags had a picture of a farmer hoeing the dirt around a plant with the caption in Portuguese, "Make It Grow."

"Isn't that a bit gutty?" asked Luciano. "People might think it's a cocoa plant."

"Not really," responded Carlos. "All most people see is a farmer fertilizing a plant. They don't see him in a vineyard or think it's a cocoa plant field. The label being in Portuguese makes them think it came from Brazil. Hey, I'm in the fertilizer business and grapes need to be fertilized. It pays well."

"As does the wine business," chimed in Giovanni.

They all laughed and Luciano's cell rang. "I must get this, it is from the local Don." Luciano stepped away speaking Italian into the phone and the conversation went on for several minutes as both Carlos and Giovanni walked over to take a closer look at the fertilizer bags. "Who would suspect they are filled with cocaine," said Carlos.

Luciano finished the call and stepped back to them, saying, "The local family is a little upset. Two of their hitmen have been killed trying to take out that CIA agent. They are using cell phone tracking technology to try and locate him. If and when they do, he will experience a very unpleasant demise."

It was like three kids with their new Christmas toy. Marcus, Martina, and Leo were in the deserted tourist parking lot just outside San Gimignano. They carefully unwrapped the package that Jenna had given Marcus and the fun began.

"I'll read the manual and the instruction sheet that Jenna put in there. You guys be the hands," said Martina.

"Look, the drone is no bigger than my hand," said Marcus as he took the drone out of its protective case.

As he extended its four propellers Martina said: "It looks like a giant black spider. Those propellers could be its front and back legs."

"What an imagination," said Leo. "Give us a break. It looks like a drone. You have seen the large ones used for surveillance."

"I know I've seen the big drones, but this looks like a little animal. Maybe not a spider. Maybe a bird or a bat. That's it. It's a bat. I'm going to call it our black bat."

"Sorry, it already has a name. It's printed on its back, Baby Elfie. See!" said Marcus as he held up the drone. Then picking up the controller, he continued with, "The controller has buttons and what looks like a mini joystick. This could be complicated. We may have a problem learning how to fly it."

Martina, picking up the user manual, commented, "It says on the front page of the manual '14+' years. You're a little older than 14, so I think you should be able to handle it." They all chuckled a bit and Leo grabbed the instruction sheet written by Jenna that was also included.

Martina continued to read the manual saying, "I think we might have an issue. They both require batteries. Dry cells for the controller, and the drone evidently has its own battery, but it has to be charged through a laptop."

"Not a problem," said Leo. "Jenna's instructions say she included charged batteries for the drone as well as AAA cells for the controller. We're good to go. She also says in the instruction sheet that Elfe will only operate from 15 to 30 minutes on a charged battery and that's why she included an additional four drone batteries, already charged. Further, she says in the instructions that you can fly Elfie with your cell phone and control its camera. The app is already installed on the cell phone she gave you. Marcus, have you got your phone with you?"

"Yes," said Marcus as he put the drone down and started getting his cell phone out of his pocket.

Martina continued thumbing through the manual, saying, "Oh, the manual in the back shows how to operate the drone and take pictures with your cell phone. This could get a little complicated."

"Yes," said Leo. "Her instructions recommend that one of us fly Elfie with the controller and somebody else use the cell phone to take pictures. Sort of a team effort. Oh well, let's give it a go."

Marcus couldn't wait. Leo was still loading batteries in the controller and Martina reading the manual when Marcus pressed the "on" switch on the Elfie's back. To his surprise, it spoke, saying, "Voice activation or remote."

"What did you say, Martina?" asked Leo.

"I didn't say a thing. That was the drone that spoke."

"You're kidding."

"Voice activation or remote."

"There it goes again. Does it say anything about voice activation in the manual? Read on, Martina."

"Yes, it does. It says we should pair the controller to the drone first. The controller's buttons and joystick override voice activation commands. The controller appears to operate like a videogame controller. No wonder they say any 14-year-old can work it.

"It goes on to say that voice activation requires its name before the command. It's sort of like the Amazon Alexa."

Overanxious Marcus, looking at Elfie, immediately said, "Elfie voice activation. Elfie, start engine." Luckily he had a good grip on Elfie as its propellers began to spin and it practically lifted out of his hand. And he quickly said, "Elfie, stop."

The first flight was something of a disaster. Elfie bounced off the pavement twice, then hit the only light pole in the vast parking lot. Marcus gave it voice commands and then tried to override them with the controller buttons and joystick.

"Marcus, you have to do better than that. We are going to be in a vineyard and then in that grove of oak trees trying to find and photograph their processing plant," said Martina.

"Let me give it a try," said Leo.

"No. Bear with me. I can get the hang of it," responded Marcus.

It took several more stops and starts, but by the third drone battery, Marcus had learned how to control the drone. Voice activation commands were either picked up by the microphone on the drone or the microphone in the controller. When the control buttons and joystick were operating, the controller microphone was muted.

During Marcus's flying attempts, both Leo and Martina were using the app or learning to use the app on Marcus's cell phone to take pictures. The app could also fly the drone as well as take pictures, but it quickly became clear that one should be the pilot and the other should be the photographer.

Marcus was flying Elfie some distance away while Martina held his cell phone and was taking both video and still pictures of its flight. Leo, standing right next to her, was also watching the cell phone screen, neither actually watching the drone until they heard Marcus yell,

"Elfie go to gravity sensing. Elfie stop. Elfie stop. Martina, Leo, I'm losing power and control. It's not responding to the controller or my voice. Watch out! It's flying towards you. It may drop to the ground before it hits you, but please try to catch it."

The encounter was quick, but in the "try to catch Elfie," Leo's body briefly caressed Martina's as they both reached for the drone and he sensed a brief spark of desire.

This was immediately muted as Elfie said, "Need charge. Need charge."

⬤

Martina filled their wine glasses as they sat around the cocktail table in their suite planning the next-day activities. Leo, looking at the map of the vineyard spread out on the table, asked, "Do we know where the vineyard tour starts?"

"Yes," answered Martina. "We pick up bicycles at the chalet where we had the wine tasting. They give us a trail map and supposedly we tour the vineyard in such a way that we arrive back at the same location."

Marcus had plugged Elfie into his laptop and they were all startled when it spoke, "I am charged, change battery. I am charged, change battery."

"Wow, it appears, besides taking flight commands, Elfie communicates to us," said Marcus.

"I don't understand," said Elfie.

"Oops, I think when it's turned on, we have to be careful about using its name as it thinks we're addressing it. It appears it's really like Amazon's Alexa. It somewhat has a mind of its own. The AI today is unbelievable," said Marcus.

"AI?" questioned Martina.

"Artificial Intelligence," answered Marcus.

"Martina, do you have Amazon Alexa here in Italy?"

"Yes. It just recently became available. I think it only has shopping list capability and weather. I don't have one and I'm not aware of any of my friends having one either."

"We've had it for a couple years in the US. It's quite fun. Has all sorts of capability. Gives you the weather, the local news, how long your commute will be. Will play your favorite songs. You can create a shopping list or a to-do list and access it on your cell phone when you're shopping. It's really pretty cool. My folks have one but I'm not sure my mother really understands it, as she tries to argue with Alexa."

Leo, still studying the map, said, "The trail goes through the oak grove on the other side of the parking lot we were in yesterday. It shows some buildings and a parking area on the other side of the grove but the trail doesn't appear to go there. Whatever is there is obviously not part of the tour. That could be the facility we're looking for. When we get to that part of our ride, that's probably where we should be flying the drone."

"Good plan," said Martina. "When videoing, we will be picking up sound too, maybe voices of people in the area."

"That could get a little dicey," said Marcus. "We have to keep the drone out of sight of anybody. Getting caught spying could be dangerous."

Martina lay in her bed contemplating what had happened in the last 24 hours. *Why had Jenna shown up?* she thought. *Her appearance ruined everything. Hell, the CIA could have sent that package by DHL. Shit, Marcus is on the couch in the sitting room and Leo's in the adjoining suite. I'm here in this giant double bed alone. I thought I wooed Marcus away from any feelings for Jenna. Her appearance obviously rekindled their relationship and I'm back in the cold. He's my ticket to the USA. I have got to get the seduction back on track. Of course, flying the drone today I think I might have kindled a little attraction from Leo. The UK isn't the USA but it still is better than here. No, I'm not going to give up on Marcus. Leo could be a fallback but Marcus is my main objective. Will see what tomorrow brings.*

CHAPTER 7

A Walk in the Woods

C arlos and Luciano were saying their goodbyes to Giovanni at the
chateau when the Agusta helicopter settled down in the landing
circle at Tenuta Toscano.

"Giovanni, you have been a wonderful host and I'm thoroughly
pleased to see that your facility will be able to accommodate my
anticipated new market," said Carlos. And with a slight smile on his
face he continued, saying, "I will increase my shipment of fertilizer to
you to facilitate the increase in your production. As soon as I have
details, I will transmit to you the shipping instructions of our wine to
our new market."

"*Grazie* and *ciao*," responded Giovanni.

Walking to the chopper, Luciano said to Carlos, "I received word
today from our local Mafia that they believe the targeted CIA agent left
the country. They were tracking his cell phone and its last location was
Livorno. They believe he might have left via the cruise ship that was in
port yesterday. They were obviously a little disappointed as the
Gambioni family promised a sizable payment had the hit been
completed.

"We have no idea what happened to the MI6 agent who was traveling with him. He may also have left. If anything changes in that area I will notify you, but I think for now our operation is safe from any discovery by authorities."

Boarding the chopper, they both waved at Giovanni.

⟐

Breakfast in San Gimignano was a planning session for Marcus, Leo, and Martina. They had commandeered one of the tables that the Leon Bianco hotel had out front in the square. A large basket of *fette biscottate* and *cornetti* with a side of apricot preserves and pots of coffee and tea dressed the table. Leo had barely enough room to lay out the map of the winery grounds showing the area they planned to visit.

"I remember looking at the bikes when we made the reservation," said Martina. "In addition to the standard bikes, they had two-seaters. Maybe we should rent one of those, so whoever's on the back seat could use the cell phone to take pictures when we're flying the drone."

"That could work," said Marcus. "Flying the drone will be easy using voice command but taking pictures will require holding the cell phone to turn on the camera and record either video or stills and to watch what we are recording."

"Oh well, I can see it now. Old Leo is about to get the short end of the stick." said Leo. "Marcus gets to ride the single bike flying the drone and Martina sits in the back of the two-seater taking pictures and not peddling very hard. Leo has to sit up front, peddling and steering. Thanks a bunch, gang."

"Well, you are so strong," said Martina with a large grin.

"Flattery gets you nowhere, Martina. You both owe me dinner tonight," responded Leo.

⟐

The Maserati purred along the curved road into the winery. The hotel had packed a delightful picnic lunch basket, which was stowed in the trunk along with a blanket. They were fully prepared for a picnic planned for somewhere along the bike trail.

"I hope the bikes we rent will have baskets to carry our picnic lunch, blanket and jackets," said Martina.

"Oh, I'm sure they will," said Leo. "And I'm sure they will be happy to sell us a bottle of wine to carry along."

"You can count on that," said Marcus. "And let's hope it's one bottled for drinking and not shipping," he continued with a smirk on his face.

"That wouldn't be totally bad," said Martina. "We would have the proof needed to solve our case, but we would all probably die before we could tell anybody. Oh well, just a thought."

"Not a very good one," said Leo.

The parking lot was sparsely populated as the trio pulled in to rent their bikes.

"Marcus, I would put the top up on the Maserati and lock it, while Martina and I go rent our bikes. I still think it's a good idea to not let anyone hear you or us speak English," said Leo as they exited the car.

"Good thought," said Marcus as he got back in the Maserati, starting the engine and initiating raising the top. "I'll unload the gear and wait out here for you."

It seemed like only a matter of minutes before Leo and Martina came back with their bikes.

"Well, look at that, matching red and white bikes. A single and a two-seater. You guys did well," said Marcus. "And both have big baskets. Looks like we're all set to go. Did they give us any clues about what we would see on the trail? Like maybe the bottling plant?" continued Marcus as he loaded their gear in the bike baskets.

"Yes and no," answered Martina. "The tour route will take us through the vineyards, an olive grove, and an oak grove. We will pass and we can stop at one of their wine cellars along the way.

The route is approximately 15 kilometers long as it winds around the vineyard and the elevation changes as there are rolling hills. About halfway through the route, we will be on top of one of the highest knolls in the vineyard and there's a little bit of a picnic area.

They suggest it is a nice stop for a picnic lunch and of course offered us a bottle of one of their special reds, which of course we bought. They did say that we would have a view of the total vineyard from there. They gave us a better map than we had and also downloaded an app on Leo's phone that works with GPS and routes you through the tour, giving you information at different points along the way."

"Oh, that says they could be tracking us," said Marcus.

"That's a possibility," said Leo, "but the other interesting thing they told us was to expect to see an occasional drone in the sky as they are used occasionally to view the grapevines. The pictures that are taken of the crop determine where more water or fertilizer is needed."

"Well, that means if we fly our drone, nobody's going to be surprised," said Marcus.

"No, not at all. We mentioned that we had a drone that we were going to use to take selfies along the way. They indicated that was certainly okay, as pictures taken by tourists help publicize the winery.

"They did show us where the bottling facility was on the map but said that they did not encourage any visitation in that area due to the trucks coming and going. Further, for hygienic reasons, visitors are not allowed in the bottling facility."

"How convenient is that for keeping things under wraps. Well, let's be off, it's exploration time. Quite frankly, I am not too encouraged on what we might see but let's give it a shot," said Marcus.

Loading their baskets, the trio set off peddling down the trail.

The Golden Duchess docked at Civitavecchia, the port for Rome. After saying goodbyes and thank you's to Captain Hempsell and the crew, Jenna debarked and boarded the bus to the Rome airport.

The nonstop flight to New York will be a long one, she thought. *The quick visit with Marcus was wonderful. Oh, if I could've only stayed.*

I hope that bitch Martina doesn't woo him away. God willing I may have saved his life by swapping his cell phone out. At least the Mafia won't be able to track him. Oh shit, they could be tracking me. I hadn't thought of that. I put the damn phone in my bag and my bag is checked on the

Duchess truck going to the airport. I hope it's turned off. I better check it before I check in for my flight.

As the trio hit a slight rise in the trail riding through the vineyards, there was a loud call from Leo. "Martina, peddle the bike. This is not a free ride. I know when you're not peddling and when you are. You can get away with it going downhill, but going up you become a big chore."

"Oh Leo, you're strong. This keeps you in shape," said Martina with a lilt in her voice.

"Don't give me that BS; do your share," responded Leo.

"We're coming to a level spot, Martina. Get my cell ready. I'm going to launch the drone," said Marcus.

All three slowed down as the drone took off and Martina started to call out what she saw.

"This is pretty cool, I can see quite a ways. Can you take it a little higher, Marcus, and just hover? Hold it right there. I'm filming now. Just try to do a slow 360 and hover. Great, great. Okay, bring her home and we'll look at the tape."

As Marcus brought the drone back, Leo laid the map out on the ground and pinpointed where they thought they were. Martina started to look at the tape on the cell phone. Marcus powered down the drone and caught it before it hit the ground, then asked, "Was I high enough that you could see over the trees that we're coming up to. It looks like an olive grove to the right of the trail."

"Yes," said Martina. "Here, look at the tape."

As she played back what was filmed on the flight, all three were glued to the little cell phone screen.

"Look, there are two buildings on the other side of that grove. Looks like our trail will take us in the opposite direction, but it would be great to get a better look at those buildings," said Martina.

"Could you make another flight with the drone just slightly above the trees and maybe get a little closer look at the buildings?" asked Leo.

"It could be pushing the distance I can fly it. But we can give it a try. I can see the drone in the sky but I can't see what it's looking at. We have to depend on the camera to do that. So when I get close, you will have to tell me, Martina. I'll then put it in hover and you hit record. I should be able to hold a position for about 10 minutes before battery requires me to bring it back. We can record and see if we get any activity going in and out. I think you have telescopic capability on the lens so we might get a little better detail than we did on the first run. Let's give it a try."

The trio was in a jubilant mood as they drove back to the hotel in San Gimignano. They felt they had had a somewhat successful day and a most enjoyable time. With the top down on the Maserati and enjoying the late afternoon warm breeze, they chatted about the day's activities.

"I think we got some great video of the building we suspect is a processing facility," said Martina. "I can't wait till we get back and recharge your cell phone so we can view the images slowly. If all goes well, it might've picked up sound because we did see workers on one of those flights."

"I wouldn't count on the sound too much," said Marcus. "But I would like a closer look at the pallets they were moving in and out of the building. We can transfer the video to the laptop and enlarge the shots when we look at them."

"I'm sure we can," said Leo. "I was looking at them when we were picnicking and then your battery went dead, followed by you knocking the wine bottle over."

"Yes. What a disaster, Marcus. I only got two sips of the wine. I was about to pour another glass."

"I'm truly sorry," said Marcus, "but it was sort of funny when you think about it. You screamed when you saw a caterpillar crossing the blanket toward your sandwich and I reached down to knock it off, hitting the wine bottle on the way. We probably can get another bottle in town. Maybe the hotel carries it."

"Ah well, these are the hazards of being sleuths in a vineyard," said Martina, and they all chuckled.

⧉

As they pulled up in front of the hotel, Leo and Martina quickly hopped out and unloaded their gear from the trunk.

"You guys take the gear up to the room and come back down and order a bottle of wine. I'll be right back. It won't take me long to park the car and a little aperitif is certainly in order before we go up and review the videos, especially if we can get a bottle of the wine that I spilled all over the picnic blanket. I'm sure the winery won't be too pleased when they open up the blanket that was carefully folded in the picnic basket that we returned," said Marcus.

⧉

Martina and Leo had just settled at a table in front of the hotel awaiting Marcus, when the local *polizia* pulled up. One officer got out and walked directly over to Martina, saying, "Signora Bufalino, *per favore*," and with his hand, directed her toward the car.

Sizing up the situation, she quickly rose from the table, saying to Leo, "Not to worry. I'll be back." She got into the back of the police car, which quickly drove away.

The Italian local police, the *polizia municipal,* usually answer directly to the mayor of the small towns where they exist. In some cases, such organizations can be infiltrated by the local Mafia, and Martina immediately sensed this. They had not driven more than a few blocks from the town square and were on a quiet side street. No words were spoken by either Martina or the officers.

Suddenly the officer sitting in the passenger seat was surprised to feel the cold steel of a gun barrel on the back of his neck. In a quiet calm voice, Martina said, "I suggest we stop right here and you explain yourselves." She said these words as she held her Walther PPK to the back of the one officer's neck and with her other hand pushed forward, she displayed her national Interpol identification.

"We don't appreciate local law enforcement meddling in our activities. I can quietly assassinate you both and report my discovery of two murdered local police found in a deserted street, or you can explain why the intrusion on my activities. Or maybe both."

"Agent Bufalino, you can't get away with this," said the officer driving the car.

"Are you willing to risk that assumption?" asked Martina as she pushed the gun barrel a little firmer into the neck of the other officer.

He immediately responded, "We were only told to find out who you were traveling with and report back. Our mayor is looking for an American who supposedly was traveling with you."

"I would suggest you report back to your mayor that if I experience any further hindrance from the municipal police, I may suggest the Anti-Mafia Investigation Department review San Gimignano's local government. I'll be getting out here," said Martina as she exited the car and walked back towards the hotel.

Coming from the parking lot and walking across the square to the hotel, Marcus was surprised to see Leo sitting alone at a table. There was a bottle of wine and glasses but no Martina. He suspected she was still in the hotel until he got closer and saw that Leo had a strange look about him.

"Leo, what is the matter? Where is Martina?" asked Marcus as he approached the table.

"They took her away," said Leo in a somewhat frustrated-sounding voice.

"What do you mean, they took her away? Who? Why?"

"The local *polizia*. She said not to worry. But really, I'm concerned."

"Is your cell charged? Let's call Agent Toscano."

Before Leo could pull his cell phone out, a black four-door Lancia Thesis pulled up in front of the hotel. Its occupant called out the window, "Marcus, Leo. Get in, quickly."

Marcus looked surprised at first, then recognizing the occupant, he called back, "Brady, what brings you here?"

"No time. Quick, both of you in the car."

Leo looked surprised and hesitant. Marcus quickly grabbed the wine bottle and Leo's arm, saying, "It's okay. I know him."

They both leaped into the car, Marcus in the passenger seat, Leo in the back and Brady drove off. "Leo, let me introduce you to Brady Nelson, senior CIA agent and Brady, please meet Leonardo Harris, MI6, who I believe you are aware of," said Marcus.

"I received word from another source that the locals were looking to question you," said Brady. "They were going to track you by picking up Martina first. It was felt that if they had that opportunity, your English would give away your identity. We couldn't let that happen. New quarters have been arranged for you at a B&B outside of town. It's run by a couple of English expats. I'll be taking you there now. You can call Martina on her cell phone. By the time we get to the B&B, I'm sure she will have been released. As I told you before, Marcus, she is an extremely resourceful and capable agent. Give her the name of the B&B and she can collect your gear from the hotel and drive the Maserati out there. Again, Marcus, don't mention my name." Then turning to Leo, Brady continued, "Leo, please have MI6 take credit for this action. Officially, I'm not here right now and I won't be able to respond to my cell phone for the next 24 to 48 hours."

Before Brady or Marcus could respond to those last remarks, the Lancia Thesis pulled off the main road into the courtyard of a sprawling farmhouse. Brady's next words were, "Quick, exit and go right in and introduce yourself. The owners know you are coming and expect you. The front door that you see goes into a smaller courtyard in front of the main entrance. I know them well and you can trust their guidance. I would go with you but I have other business. *Ciao*."

With that interchange, the Lancia sped away. Standing with Marcus in front of the farmhouse door and looking perplexed, Leo said, "Marcus, what just happened?"

"I'm not really sure myself, but let me explain what I do know. Brady is a senior CIA agent, supposedly over here on a secret mission. He was made aware of our presence and mission and instructed to keep an eye on us when he could without compromising his mission, whatever that is. He introduced himself to me when we first arrived in San Gimignano and now this is the first I've seen or heard from him since then. We better go on in and meet our hosts."

Marcus and Leo were seated at the pool sipping the wine they had brought. The B&B that Brady had brought them to was a wonderful restored Tuscan farmhouse located in the hamlet of Libbiano just 8 kilometers out of San Gimignano. It could accommodate up to 12 guests in a combination of nine double rooms and suites. Due to the off season, it was closed to tourists for refurbishment of some of the rooms and their hosts indicated that the planned reopening was not scheduled for another month. Thus, the entire place was their own. Further, after introductions the managing couple assured them that in addition to breakfast, they would be more than willing to provide any additional meals they desired. The wife explained that during the season she ran cooking classes for their guests.

"Leo, what a place. This beautiful and colorful garden surrounding a swimming pool bordered with a grass lawn is so appealing, and look at the panoramic view. We should have stayed here when we arrived," said Marcus.

"I agree. The decor inside is not too shabby either. Antique furniture, local artwork, and rooms with modern plumbing. Fabulous. But remember, we didn't have much of a choice," responded Leo.

"Martina had made her mind up where we were going to stay and that was that. This place is actually a little closer to the winery. Oh well, we're here now, so let's enjoy it. It's probably a little more secure than being in town."

"By the way, do you have any idea why Brady doesn't want Martina to know he exists? I don't have a problem with it and I can certainly say that MI6 rescued us, but I'm sort of curious."

"I have no idea," said Marcus. "As I said, he met me the first day we were here. Actually showed me where the hotel parking lot was. He briefly introduced himself and gave me his cell phone number saying to call if we needed help. He obviously knew Martina as he told me she was quite capable, but he didn't want her to know of his existence. Jenna did tell me earlier that there was another CIA agent in the area active on another classified activity. But that's all I know." Their conversation and the tranquility of the surroundings was interrupted by the obvious sound of a rumbling sports car engine coming from the square in front of the farmhouse.

"Ah, Martina has arrived," said Leo.

"Yes, and I can't wait to hear how she dealt with the police," said Marcus.

Brady made it to the desired parking lot outside the walls of San Gimignano in record time and it was only a short walk to tower building 14. For lack of a better name, that's what he called the facility he was headed for. The digital combination lock on the door responded to his fingers, and he was inside facing an elevator. He pushed the button and the door opened. Here he pressed the button labeled AISE, code for *Agencia Informazioni e Sicurezza Esterna,* the External Intelligence and Security Agency of Italy. The elevator door opened to a room filled with computers and screens on the wall depicting locations around the world.

"Brady, wonderful. You're right on time. I think you Americans must have a clock in your head, at least you do. You never miss a scheduled appointment," said the other lone agent in the facility.

"Lorenzo, you set a time, and I'm here. That's just the way I am," replied Brady.

"I assume your call meant our mission is scheduled?"

"Yes, a chopper will pick us up in the deserted tour bus parking lot precisely at midnight. I apologize that scheduling took so long, but the Holy City has a very active schedule and we want our mission to be accomplished when it's least populated. Tonight's the night.

Our inside contact you are scheduled to meet will take you where the migrating birds are being held. You will have approximately an hour to count noses, take pictures, talk, whatever you want for your mission. Following, we will be lifted out by the chopper and return here.

By the way, you told me your mission is called CMV. Can you tell me what that stands for?"

"Certainly," said Brady with a slight smile. "You're cleared and you're helping us. CMV is short for cardinal migration verification."

"This isn't an extraction mission, is it? We didn't plan for that."

"No, not at all. We just want to count noses to validate what we surmised, that the disappearance of the indicted from the US was planned and executed by the Vatican."

CHAPTER 8

Libbiano

Their B&B hostess prepared a delicious meal, which was enjoyed by all. The sun was slowly going down but it was still quite warm and an evening swim was thought to be perfect for relaxation. Marcus and Leo were the first in the pool and after a brief swim the length of the pool, they stood in the shallow end.

"I don't know where the heater is but this pool temperature is perfect," said Leo.

"Yes, it's almost like a bathtub," said Marcus.

Martina finally arrived carrying an armload of towels, which she parked in one of the chaise lounges surrounding the pool. Pulling off her cover-up, displaying a beautiful figure barely covered by a brief bikini, she performed a perfect dive into the deep end.

Leo's eyes expanded to the size of saucers, and all he could say was, "Wow."

"Yes, Martina cuts a classic figure," said Marcus. "I was pretty lucky on my last assignment, accompanied by three extremely attractive women."

"Three?" questioned Leo. "I see Martina. I met Jenna. Who was the third?"

"Angelina Gambioni, daughter of Franco Gambioni, Don of the Gambioni family, the most notorious of the five Mafia families in New York. Also the principal of my last assignment. Posing as newlyweds on the cruise, Jenna and I befriended the Gambioni family and became quite close. I'll tell you, in addition to being extremely attractive, Angelina is smart, has excellent martial arts capability and can be ruthless. She killed an adversary in San Juan. Two thugs were trying to kidnap her and they soon learned she was not to be messed with."

Completing her dive, Martina came up right between Marcus and Leo saying, "What a delight and were you two talking about me?"

"No," said Marcus. "I was describing Angelina to Leo."

"I have to admit she is very attractive, friendly, approachable but as cold and calculating as they come," responded Martina. "By the way, according to your FBI, Marcus, Franco is in the pen and Angelina supposedly is running the organization. It's amazing that the other four Don's in the area accept her. That's definitely not Mafia standard operating practice. Women are normally shielded from all the organized crime activities."

"Oh, really, I wasn't aware of that," responded Marcus. "After we turned the information over to the FBI, the CIA was out of it. I'm glad to hear Franco is in prison. I'm sure he was responsible for the condo explosion that almost killed Jenna."

"I'm sure you're right," continued Martina. "The rumble over here is that he is the one financing the hit on you with the local Mafia. He wasn't too happy at the end of the cruise when he found out you both were CIA."

"Hey mates, a temperate evening calls for a cool digestif. Limoncello, anyone?"" came the call from the other end of the pool interrupting the discussion of Marcus"'s past assignment.

"Who is that?" asked Martina.

"Oh, you didn't meet him? That's Gordon, our host," said Leo.

"I only met Abigail when I arrived and of course at dinner. So Gordon is the husband?"

"Yes, and he is great," said Marcus. "He is retired, MI6. They are originally from Newcastle and bought this place seven years ago."

"When did you find all this out?"

"We were here quite a while before you arrived and our MI6 contact explained this on the drive out," said Leo.

"Well, I'm for limoncello," said Marcus, as he pushed both Martina and Leo down in the water and swam to the other end.

The limoncello bottle had been drained and their hosts had long ago taken their leave. Martina, wrapped in towels and complaining about getting cold, finally said her goodnights and went off to bed. As soon as she was gone, Leo said, "Marcus, we have to talk. I realize we are supposed to stay professional on these assignments, but this is the first time I've worked with a female agent on the team. I don't know what you guys do in the US but I feel I'm becoming emotionally involved and I don't think that's good. Having emotions involved in role-playing may be great in an acting career but could be dangerous in our line of work. What do you do?"

"Quite frankly, it's difficult. I assume you're talking about Martina. Well, I'll admit it gets complicated. On my last assignment I spent ten days posing as newlyweds with Jenna and there's no question that at the end of those ten days, we were as close to being a couple as you could get. Quite frankly, I still have strong feelings for her. Now about here and now and Martina. I don't know, she's a huge emotional question mark. She obviously is a flirtatious individual. Maybe that's just the Italian in her. There is no question when she role-plays she appears to want to go all the way. That was obvious when we arrived in San Gimignano. I take it you're developing feelings for her."

"Well, yes, I think I am."

"Well, personally, I have no problem with that. As I told you, I still have strong feelings for Jenna. Martina is just a team member and we're trying to do a job. Professionally I have a problem with it and I have a problem with myself. You know from your training and I know from my training, emotion can inhibit your actions on dangerous assignments. That's about all I can say. I think we just have to leave it there. If you have feelings for Martina, go for it, but just don't let it impact our assignment."

Brady and Lorenzo were early to the deserted parking lot and continued to chat while waiting for the chopper.

"How's the junior CIA agent that you're watching over?" asked Lorenzo.

"Well, their mission is getting a little dicey. It involves both the Sicilian Mafia as well as the local Mafia and there's a mark out on him, evidently generated by a US Mafia family in New York."

"Wow, is he in danger? Is there anything we should be doing?"

"For now, I think he's okay. He is teamed with a young MI6 agent and also with the Italian Interpol agent I talked about."

"Oh, the one you think is your daughter."

"Well, yes. We were all young once. Years ago, I was on assignment in Italy and again teamed with one of your agencies, and I had an affair with the girl I was teamed with. At the end of the mission, she told me that she was married and she also thought she was pregnant. We went our separate ways. Through the years, however, we occasionally corresponded: you know, the family Christmas cards, etc. A couple years after our meeting, she did have another child, a boy. I followed the progress of the girl in the annual Christmas cards. She has become highly educated, speaking several languages, and ultimately went into Interpol, where I believe she's one of their key agents."

"Does she know about you? Have you met her?"

"I really don't know if her mother ever told her about me. She probably just figures I'm some friend her mother used to know and keeps contact with because I'm American. I briefly saw her in San Gimignano when I waylaid Marcus, the young CIA agent, on his way to the hotel parking lot. But other than that . . ."

Batabatabatabatabata. Their conversation was interrupted by the whirring of the chopper as it landed in the parking lot.

Breakfast was normally served on the patio at the B&B. It was an expansive covered area at the back of the farm house overlooking the pool. Marcus and Martina were surprised to see Leo and their host, Gordon, already seated at the large round table located at one end. They had a huge map laid out on the table in addition to two mugs of tea.

"Good morning," said Leo, as they approached the table. Holding up his mug he continued, "It's so great to have good dark breakfast tea in the morning. What a treat."

"Your English background is showing," commented Martina.

Just then Abigail approached from the kitchen carrying two mugs and a giant pot, saying,

"I'm sure you two would prefer coffee. Please sit down."

"Yes, please join us," called out Gordon as he folded up the map that they were looking at. "We were reviewing a somewhat detailed map of the area I have. It shows many of the roads and lanes that are not depicted on commercial maps available at car rental offices. There appears to be a back road fairly close to our farmhouse that enters the vineyard property. The south border of their property is really quite close to us. I suspect that it is the road used for delivery and shipping. The map does show some structures just inside their property line that could be the buildings you filmed with your drone. I have never been down that road but I would guess there is a locked gate to the vineyard there. It would probably be opened and closed by vineyard personnel when trucks were entering or leaving. I doubt that it's guarded."

"That's great!" said Marcus. "Maybe we can sneak in and get a closer look at the buildings."

"Well, before you do that, I would suggest you fly your drone from the public part of the road and get some better pictures. I'm sure there's very little if any traffic on that back road except vineyard trucks," responded Gordon.

"We have bicycles here that we rent to our guests. You're more than welcome to use them to get down there. I'd say it can't be much more than a mile or a mile and a half from here. I'm sorry, I get used to talking in miles, but everything is in kilometers here. I'd say it's about 2 kilometers."

"I believe another picnic in the area is to be on our schedule today," said Martina with a big smile, and looking at Abigail, she asked, "Is a picnic lunch a possibility?"

"I'm not sure there's a place for it on that road," commented Gordon, "but having it along might be a good idea. Anyone seeing you would just assume you're tourists, exploring the countryside by bike."

"Martina, I have baskets in the kitchen. I often fix lunches for our guests. I'm sure we will be able to put a suitable lunch together for the three of you," said Abigail.

Marcus and Leo accompanied Gordon out to the shed where he stored the inn's bicycles. "I have ten of them out here," he said as he led them out the front door over to the adjoining shed. "The bikes are hung in the shed to minimize weight on the tires while stored. We can get three down, clean them up and check the tires. They have been out there for four months during our renovation; the tires probably need air."

As they left, Martina followed Abigail into the kitchen, saying, "What can I do to help?"

"Oh great, follow me. Between the two of us we will have a picnic lunch made in no time."

"You know how many times I've been to Tuscany, and I've never been to this particular area. The small town I passed through as I drove here is intriguing," said Martina.

"That's Libbiano. And yes, it is a delightful area. You'd be surprised that many of the restored farmhouses around here are either owned or in some cases rented by ex-pats from the US or the UK. Many are writers and some artists. Some are only here for the summer and their places are closed during the winter months. It's a delightful community. I don't want to distract you from your mission, but please, enjoy the sights on your bike ride today. You should see some interesting homes along the way. Many were constructed during the Renaissance. As such, restoration is constrained by laws preventing modification of external appearance. They look just as they looked 400 years ago. You may not be aware but an American novelist wrote a book about restoring a farmhouse here back in the '90s. I keep a copy of it in the bookcase in the living area. The house she wrote about restoring is actually in this area. That book was published 20 years ago and it still inspires tourists to visit the area."

"That's interesting. I thought the wineries and the historic cities like San Gimignano and Pisa were the big draw."

"All those aspects contribute to making this one of the most popular tourist areas in the country. I believe after Rome and Venice, this area is the preferred destination."

It was then that Martina switched to her investigative questioning. "By the way, you emigrated here, purchased property and are now running a business. Have you ever had any interface with the local Mafia?" she asked.

"Well, not directly, but close friends of ours were publicly objecting to a city project involving a public swimming pool planned to be built close to their property. One morning they found an old WW II hand grenade in their mailbox and a note suggesting they cease any public objections. Obviously, some sort of organized crime-backed activity. I'm not aware of the tentacles from Sicily extending into the area. But as you know, probably better than I, all is possible in this country and organized crime in some form always seems to exist."

The conversation went back to the ingredients going into the picnic lunch, but Martina's mind began to spin. *I'm beginning to think Gordon and Abigail are a little more aware of organized crime in the area than what they're revealing. And how did MI6 know this would be a safe area for us to be located? I'm beginning to suspect my foreign associates. Do Marcus and Leo have knowledge and contacts that they're not sharing with me?*

⦿

Gordon opened the shed door and flipped on the lights. Marcus and Leo gazed at the ten bikes neatly hung from the rafters. "Oh, you have Galletti bikes. They are like what they had at the winery," said Marcus.

"What's so special about them? I'm sure they exist in the US, but I haven't seen them."

"They are the "Cicli Galetti Trail/Gravel bikes," responded Gordon, "probably the premier trail bikes made in Italy. Very popular and very expensive, but extremely durable. They can stand up to the worst environment and treatment applied by any rider. The five in the back have baskets; let's get three of those down."

After cleaning up the bikes and checking their tires, they were wheeling them back to the front of the farmhouse when Marcus said, "Gordon, please don't mention Brady in front of Martina. For some reason he just doesn't want her to know about his existence. So as far as she's concerned, we were brought here by an MI6 contact, name not to be mentioned, because he obviously doesn't exist."

"That's not a problem," responded Gordon. "Abigail doesn't know who brought you because she wasn't home when Brady brought you over, and she never asked me about it. Any idea why the charade?"

"Not really. Brady was somewhat secretive about it. I'm sure we'll find out eventually."

◉

It was a rainy morning in New York but Jenna didn't mind her commute. She had just returned from an exciting brief trip to the Mediterranean, visited friends on the Golden Duchess and best of all, seen Marcus at a winery in Italy. She couldn't wait to get to work to tell her boss about the trip, particularly the related details that she learned about the case that Marcus and Leo of MI6 were working on.

Exiting the subway in downtown Manhattan and crossing the street, she rushed to enter the office building housing the CIA. Off the elevator on the tenth floor she quickly settled in her cubicle. She no sooner had taken off her raincoat and hung it up, when over the PA system came,

"Jenna, report."

The one thing she'd had difficulty getting used to was her boss using the PA system instead of the phone. Booming again over the cubicles came, "Jenna, now."

She exited her cubicle and rushed to her boss's office. As she entered, in a very stern voice he said, "Sit down. Would you mind explaining yourself? When you returned to work after your accident, you had a simple assignment. Review routine background checks on UN personnel and maintain contact with Agent Peterson on assignment with MI6. And that was purely to provide any travel assistance he might need while working in the UK. It was a routine assignment. You initially performed it well. All of a sudden you take a leave of absence, I get calls from our contacts in Europe, a bill for four days on a cruise ship, and a cockamamie story about cocaine being shipped in wine bottles. What the hell's going on?"

Jenna, a bit flustered at first, settled down and related her story: what she had experienced in Italy on her brief trip and what she learned from Marcus, Agent Harris, and Agent Bufalino. At first her boss had a somewhat dubious and questioning look on his face but it gradually changed to serious and intense.

When she finished he responded with, "Even though Agent Nelson is working on a highly classified international political issue, I'm sure he can deal with Marcus's safety better than anything we can do from here. In regards to the cocaine, I'm not sure you have enough data to go to the FBI. Considering the number of container ships and the quantity of containers arriving in New York, how would you inspect them, and really, what would you be looking for? This could get really complicated and extremely expensive considering the number of agents that may be required. We've got to get more data on what's going on before we alert the FBI. I'm afraid with what you've got, we'd look a little ridiculous in suggesting they move out on this.

"The operation is a little dicey in Europe working with MI6, Interpol, and the Italian Anti-Mafia Investigation Department. We don't really get to call the shots, even though we have an agent involved. Let's let this evolve a little further before we get the FBI involved. Keep me informed of any future developments and no wild expenditures without approval."

She thanked her boss, exited his office, and started back to her cubicle. Recognizing that an official report to the FBI was not to be made at this time, she decided that a quick call to a close friend she had over there was in order. She was just curious as to what was going on with the Gambioni family, if anything.

Detouring to the break room, she was happy to find it empty. Pulling out her cell phone, she called her friend, who answered immediately and she said, "Hi Fred, Just a quick call. Anything new on the Gambioni family?"

"Well briefly, it's this," responded Fred. "The appeal filed by Franco's consigliere was rejected, so he is still in prison. Informants indicate his daughter Angelina is running the family. Very contrary to local Mafia operations, however, we feel Franco is really calling the shots from prison. We know they have drugs on the street and we are pretty sure they are coming from Colombia but we haven't been able to determine how they're getting them into the country."

"Give us some time," said Jenna. "We may be able to help you. We have an activity going on in Italy that may shed some light on things. Can't talk now officially but will get back to you soon.

Thanks much. Got to go."

Her phone went quickly back into her pocket and she exited the break room.

The ride on the back road through the rolling hills of Tuscany was as pleasurable as predicted by Abigail. The three bikers commandeered the road and Martina was obviously captivated by the sites, calling out to Leo and Marcus as they rounded each bend in the road, "Oh, look over there, that farmhouse. Look over there, how they terraced the hillside, the grape vines look like they're on steps. Oh, up on that hill. That farmhouse, looks like a miniature old world castle."

"Martina, be careful. Keep your eyes on the road. there are some rough areas up ahead," called out Marcus.

Rounding the next bend, they came upon a long straight stretch going slightly downhill. The right of the road continued along the terraced hillside while the left leveled out to a plain that was totally covered with grape vines.

"I bet that's the beginning of the Toscano vineyard," called out Leo.

"Yes, I think you're right. Look further down the road where those cypress trees are. It looks like there's a gate and a road into the property," said Marcus.

As they got closer, they spotted a young woman struggling with a bicycle on the side of the road next to the cypress trees.

"Looks like someone is in trouble," called out Martina.

"Yes, let's see if we can help," said Marcus as all three speeded up to get to her.

As they pulled up, all three were surprised to see the girl was Natalie Toscano, Giovanni Toscano's daughter who had conducted the wine tasting event they had attended.

"Natalie, what happened? Can we help?" asked Leo.

"Oh please, if you can. You know my name! Do I know you?"

"We attended a wine tasting with you two days ago. How did this happen?" said Leo.

"I was coming down the road and shifted and hit a bump in the road at the same time. The chain popped off and I went off the road into this tree. I'm fine but my bike sure isn't."

"Let's see. If it's not broken, we can get it back on," said Leo.

"What are you doing alone down on this back road? You have those beautiful bike trails all through your vineyard. We were on them just yesterday."

"You're right, and that's why I'm here. It's my little escape from the tourists that visit the winery. My standard ride is out the front gate around the perimeter of the vineyard and back in on the service gate just down the road a piece. It's about 15 kilometers. It's sort of a requirement to maintain my figure when you consider the food that can be consumed in the wine tastings."

While Natalie was rambling on about her lifestyle, Martina's mind was spinning, *I'm sure the Toscano family is a typical Italian Mafia family,* she thought. *Natalie probably knows absolutely nothing about the cocaine/wine impregnation. A test question or two will validate that.*

She then said, "Natalie, where does the service road go?"

"It goes to our bottling and shipping facility. From there, there's a golf-cart road that goes back up to the tasting rooms. I used to stop in the bottling facility and chat with the staff there but a year ago there was some sort of an accident. My father told me it was too dangerous for me to be in there and that I wouldn't be allowed in anymore."

As I expected, thought Martina.

"I'm so happy you came along," said Natalie. "This road is seldom used. In fact, it actually dead-ends 4 kilometers past our gate. What were you doing on it? I don't believe it's on many maps." Natalie paused for a minute, then before anyone could answer, she said, "I remember you now. You were part of the cruise ship tour. What are you doing here now?"

Martina's mind went into overdrive. *Oh shit, how do we explain ourselves? We can't tell her who we really are.*

Marcus had similar thoughts. *What do I do now? If I speak at all she will know I'm American. Do we continue our charade?*

Their thinking was interrupted and they were both surprised with Leo's quick response. "I'm sorry, I guess we didn't introduce ourselves at the wine tasting," he said. "We work for Tuscany Tours in Livorno. We handle many of the shore excursions for the different cruise ships. We're back in the area in search of new excursion possibilities. We are actually staying locally in Libbiano for a few days."

Wow, smart response, Leo, thought Marcus, *but I don't think I'll say anything for the moment.*

Martina's mind continued to spin also as she thought, *Clever response, Leo. Let's see if we can capitalize on it.* And she said, "Since you live here in the area, Natalie, do you have any suggestions?"

"Well yes, we do have other things available at the winery besides wine tasting. You obviously are aware of the bike riding activity you participated in yesterday. We also offer a truffle hunt in our oak grove where you can go off the beaten path in search of those delicacies. We provide dogs that sniff out the truffles. It makes a nice outing because it's down by the Elsa River. This can be followed with a culinary class utilizing the truffles."

"That sounds pretty interesting, but is there anything else available to tour associated with the winemaking?" asked Martina.

Good question, Martina, thought Marcus. *Maybe we get an invite to where we really want to be.*

"Well, you can tour our wine cellars, which house the oak barrels where the wine maturation process is completed. This can be combined with a dinner or lunch. Also, close by is our fermentation room. I'm not sure touring that would be very exciting. Just a bunch of stainless steel tanks," responded Natalie.

"By the way did your host, wherever you're staying, mention the *sagra del vino* that starts tomorrow?"

"What's that?" asked Leo.

"Oh, I'm sorry. You're obviously English by your accent. Well, all the small towns in Tuscany have festivals celebrating different foods during the season. There are *sagre* for cherries, chestnuts, wild boar, olive oil, you name it, and of course wine. In addition to booths with different local wines, the local restaurants will be offering suggested food pairings for the wines. There will be entertainment and dancing. It's all great fun and takes place in the piazza. The Toscano winery will have a booth, which I will be manning with my sister as well as some of our staff. It's tomorrow night and starts about sundown. You should definitely come by. I'll make sure I have some winery brochures, and of course I'll have some wine for you to taste."

Looking at her watch and then Leo, she continued, "Oh dear, am I good to go? I have a tasting I'm supposed to host in an hour."

"You have a sister?" questioned Martina, and Leo quickly said, "You're good to go. I popped the chain back on the sprocket. You will be fine. And we will definitely come to the *sagra* tomorrow. Did I pronounce that right?"

"Yes, you did, and thank you all so much. Yes, I do have a sister and you might meet her tomorrow. I must hurry; the back gate is normally locked, but when I leave the winery out the front gate, I tell the guards when to expect me and they send someone down to open the gate. I dare not miss him."

With that, she hopped on her bike and was off down the road.

"Wow, Leo, that was great. Quick thinking," said Martina. "I better call Sophia and tell her what you said, just in case Natalie should call Tuscan Tours to confirm your story. I don't think she will but we better be prepared."

"Yeah, that was great," said Marcus. "I didn't speak at all as I wasn't sure who I am." Then looking at Martina, he continued, "Am I still your Italian husband or can I be myself? Somewhere along the line I'm going to have to speak, especially if we meet her at the festival tomorrow night. And if I do, she's going to know I'm American."

"Good point," said Martina. "I think I turned off the local Mafia with my discussion with the San Gimignano police. Maybe we can get some guidance from Gordon when we get back home. I'm sure he can tell us about the festival and who we can expect to be there. I don't think there will be a problem with Natalie. From my questions to her and her answers I sense this is a typical Italian family and that the women are totally shielded from any Mafia connections that may exist."

"Martina, hold on," said Marcus. "I know you're from Palermo and I respect your Interpol background, but I think you're totally off base. This is the twenty-first century and the world has definitely changed and that's certainly true with organized crime. Look, we both experienced it on the last assignment we worked together. I don't believe Angelina is the exception. I truly believe that today's Mafia millennial women are getting involved in the family operation and are no longer being sheltered."

Then turning his attention to Leo, he said, "It was a great story you told Natalie but I don't think she believed a word of it. And she almost told you she didn't. Remember, she said this was an unmarked road and dead-ended shortly past the vineyard back gate. What would tour representatives be doing on it? There definitely wouldn't be any shore excursion opportunities on such a road.

"Oh, she played along, but she really sensed something was awry. I don't think she suspects who we are, but she definitely doesn't believe what you told her. And I believe she thinks we're some sort of a threat and that's why she wanted to quickly leave and inform somebody. Either her father or someone on the staff or both. That story she told about having to get back to do a wine tasting obviously wasn't true. They are always scheduled around the noon hour, primarily to provide time for selling wine to the tour groups before their tour buses have to leave."

Turning back to Martina, he continued, "Further, I wouldn't give too much credibility to that story she told about the bottling facility."

"Marcus, if what you say is true, I would suggest that any activity that we had planned for their back gate and this general area should be put on hold," said Leo, "especially flying our drone. In fact, I think we should turn around and ride back up the road and select another area to have our picnic. We've got a lot to contemplate here. A new plan is definitely in order."

As they went to their bikes, Leo continued, saying, "I'm sure by now Natalie has informed someone of our presence and I wouldn't be a bit surprised to see one of their crop surveillance drones come our way to watch us." With that comment, they all looked up and, as if on command, spotted a small black drone circling above the cyprus trees.

Collectively, they said, "Oh, shit."

Martina was in the kitchen with Abigail. She insisted on helping with dinner, primarily because she wanted to learn how to make the dish that Abigail was preparing, a staple of Tuscany: rabbit with tomatoes and balsamic vinegar.

Leo and Marcus sat on the veranda with Gordon, sipping wine and excitingly describing the plan they had come up with. Leo had contacted MI6 in London earlier and was assured that Gordon Smith could be trusted. Further, he was told that, though retired due to his current residency in Italy, he is still used occasionally as a consultant. As such, they felt it important to brief him and get some guidance.

As they described their plan, Gordon interrupted and said, "Gentlemen, slow down. I think you better give me a little more background."

"Well, we were sent over here to participate with the Italian Central Directorate for Anti-Drug Services. They had an open ongoing investigation of cocaine trafficking in the country," said Leo.

"The rumble is that the Calisto cartel in Colombia has cut a deal with the Sicilian Mafia to funnel their cocaine to the US, UK and France through Italy," chimed in Marcus. "How it's getting into Italy and how it's getting out and who's involved is the issue at hand. We were assigned as a team to assist the directorate in their investigation."

"Interesting," said Gordon. "How does that bring you here?"

"Shortly after we arrived in Venice, the department called us in on a case where a tourist died of an overdose. It was determined that the cocaine she consumed was infused in wine. That opened the door to the possibility that the cocaine was being transported out of Italy in wine. We traced the source of the wine that the tourists consumed to this winery," said Leo. "It appears that authorities in Italy do not make raids on facilities unless they have positive proof that a criminal activity is being conducted there. Thus, our job is to determine if and how cocaine is getting into this winery as suspected, and if it's being shipped out infused in wine," he continued.

"Oh, and to make life interesting," injected Marcus, "we were informed that a local Mafia family has been contracted by the Gambioni family in New York to take me out." That statement caused Gordon to briefly choke on his wine. "So now that you know the background, what do you think of the plan we came up with today?" It was an emotional delivery and one could sense anxiety in their voices.

Gordon listened intently to their discussion and appeared captivated by the story. As they finished, he said nothing. Looking at them both, he just sat there stroking his chin. Then in a somewhat calming voice, he said, "It has possibilities, but I suggest a little modification. First, Abigail accompanies Martina and Leo into town. She is well known in town and she's also known to bring our houseguests in and introduce them around. It's part of our normal B&B package and sort of expected.

It's a small town and the local vendors are always interested in seeing our out-of-town guests. Regardless of what Natalie thinks, the townspeople will consider Abigail ushering Martina and Leo around as totally normal. Further, she can explain to Natalie if asked, Marcus, that your absence is due to the laryngitis you experienced from that cold you had when you arrived and that walking around at night wouldn't be the best for it."

"Great idea," said Leo, "and I'm sure I'm not the first Brit that Abigail has shown the town to."

"That's right. Now, Marcus, about your escapade. I think that also has possibilities. You're right in assuming that most of the staff at the winery will be at the festival as it's one of the highlighted events for the locals. But making a night visit to the winery by yourself is not too swift. I will accompany you. Quite frankly, you'd be totally lost on these roads at night. Further, I'm retired but I still have some equipment from my professional days and that includes night vision goggles. Also, I'm sure you noticed in the shed the two Vespas we have. The bicycles are for our guests; we use the Vespas to run about, and we will use them for our little safari tonight.

Though Tuscany Tours validated the story Natalie heard from the three bikers who helped her at the back gate, she still felt uneasy about it. *It just seems so strange,* she thought. *One of them never spoke at all, and the conversation with the other two just didn't make sense. That back road doesn't go anywhere except to our back gate and it dead-ends just a ways past it. Were they lost? I think I better talk to my dad.*

Giovanni listened intently to Natalie's story, then bursting into a smile, he said, "Natalie, not to worry. The pictures taken by our crop surveillance drone, that you ordered when you returned, shows them going back up the same road and stopping for a picnic. All quite normal with what they told you. Go to the *sagra*; if they show up, give them some brochures."

As he said these words, his mind had other thoughts. *I think I might call my cousin in Venice. We haven't spoken since the family reunion five years ago and I know he is with one of the investigative departments in the government, I'm not sure which, and I definitely wouldn't want him aware of our new operation. But I might just get some general information relative to any possible government investigations going on in the area. There's an outside possibility that Natalie's concerns are warranted.*

CHAPTER 9

Toscano Surveillance

"You're in for a real treat," said Abigail as they prepared to ride their bikes into town. Parking could be a real problem, so she had insisted that they go by bike. "In addition to the booths of the wineries and restaurants, the inhabitants of the village prepare and serve typical local dishes outside their homes.

"Oh, and I'm not a dancer but you two could be in for another treat. There is always a local band in the piazza playing dance music, starting about seven, and continuing to who knows how long. It will really be great."

"This could be real fun. Are we dressed okay for the occasion?" asked Martina.

"You both look fine, dressed as typical tourists. You both are in for a fun and exciting experience," said Abigail. Little did she know how exciting it would turn out and how fun it would not be.

They approached the outskirts of Libbiano in fewer than 20 minutes. Locking their bikes at a bike stand just inside town, they proceeded on foot. They had barely passed the first food stand when the calls came out. "Please, Mrs. Smyth, have your guests try this."

All conversation was in local Italian, so Leo had a little difficulty understanding.

Martina had no problem and said, "Abigail, you must be known by everybody."

"Well, no, not everybody, but certainly many. I am usually encouraging my guests to taste the various dishes as they truly represent the typical local cuisine. And quite frankly, taking my guests to this event saves me from having to cook a meal." They all chuckled as she continued, "This alley that we're on opens up to a wider street. I'm sure we will find the Toscano winery booth there with Natalie. By the way, I've never met her. You two can introduce me. This could be good. She could maybe tell some of her winery visitors about our B&B. I brought some business cards along which I will pass on to her."

"Is that such a good idea?" asked Leo. "That would pretty much announce to her where we are staying. I thought when Brady brought us out from San Gimignano, your place was supposed to be somewhat of a safe place."

"I doubt if Natalie's aware of the mark on Marcus by the local Mafia in San Gimignano," answered Abigail. "Further, you just being with me here pretty much announces where you're staying. We will just have to accept the risk to follow through with your tour guide story."

Their conversation was interrupted by the noise level of the crowd as the alley they were walking in widened to the width of a street. There were booths on both sides and a considerable number of people. A band was playing in the distance, echoing off the buildings of the town. As the three entered the crowded area, Leo affectionately grabbed Martina's hand and she responded with a slight squeeze.

"Look, some of the women are in costume; they have embroidered skirts and bodices," said Martina.

"Yes, and that's not unusual. That's traditional Tuscan dress and they usually don it at the festivals. You will even see some with elaborate hats decorated with flowers and fruit. It's all part of the celebration," said Abigail.

"Oh, there's the Toscano winery booth across the road," she continued, as she grabbed Leo's hand and pulled him and Martina through the crowd to the opposite side of the street. The booth was well decorated with flowers and a large Tenuta Toscano banner. There was a counter held up by two oak wine casks and a back rack filled with wine bottles. That young woman in the booth, I don't recognize her but she has a striking outfit. The embroidery is gorgeous."

Looking up, Leo said, "That's Natalie. Good, she is here. I can introduce you."

As they approached the booth, Natalie smiled and called out, "Great of you to come. I have your brochures here. Where's your silent friend?"

"He is still suffering from laryngitis and a cold," responded Leo. "He thought the night air might not be the greatest and decided to stay back at the B&B and get some rest. But here, let me introduce you to our host. This is Abigail Smyth. She and her husband run the B&B where we are staying."

Abigail and Natalie immediately got into a discussion about her B&B and how Natalie might be able to recommend it to visitors at the winery. While this discussion ensued, Leo and Martina began tasting some of the wines that were on display at the Toscano booth. Natalie then turned to Martina and Leo, saying, "I'm so glad you came along and helped me yesterday. If you hadn't, I would've had to limp down to our gate with my broken bike. I don't know how I would've done it."

"Well, I guess you are a lucky pup, Natalie," said Leo, "as quite frankly, I don't know how we got on that road. We were literally lost, and after getting you up and rolling again, we went back the way we came. I guess all things work out for the best."

Well, maybe my father was right, thought Natalie. *I guess they really were scouting for places for Tuscany Tours. However, Martina is obviously Italian but Leo is certainly not.* Then turning to Leo, she asked, "How did you get involved with Tuscany Tours? You are obviously not from Italy."

"That's easy. The customers of Tuscany Tours are primarily American and English cruise lines. They often hire English-speaking tour guides both from the US and the UK. I also speak Italian, as it was my mother's native language.

Well done. I think Leo has her convinced we're not a threat, thought Martina as she gave Leo's hand another squeeze and gazed at him with a smile and affectionate and proud look in her eyes.

Deftly observing Martina's reaction to Leo's dialogue, Abigail said to them both, "I hear the music. I think you two should go to the piazza for dancing. I'll catch up with you there. I have more to discuss with Natalie and there are a few other vendors I want to talk to. Go enjoy."

⊕

As predicted, the back gate to the Tuscany winery was locked, and no one was there guarding it. Gordon and Marcus, dressed in dark clothing, parked their motor scooters next to the gate and walked around on to the winery lane. Typical of vineyards, there were no fences around the property at large so other than the gate and possibly 25 meters of fencing on either side, access was easily available on foot. "This lane should take us to the bottling facility and probably a large parking lot to accommodate shipping vehicles. I doubt whether the facility is manned at night and especially tonight. I would expect the entire staff is off to the festival," said Gordon.

"These night vision goggles are fantastic," said Marcus. "There are no lights and the moon isn't up yet, but I can still see quite well."

"Yes, with these infrared stealth goggles, you can see quite clearly up to 50 feet ahead. You probably won't believe this, but they are not MI6 issue. I got these on Amazon from your country."

"Oh, I believe you. Amazon is unbelievable. I don't think there's anything you can order that they don't have or have access to. I just didn't realize they delivered out of the country."

The lane turned right and entered a small grove of oak trees, then exited into a large parking area. At the far end was a large gray building that appeared to have steel siding with no windows. A large garage-type door that was not completely shut faced the parking lot. As they were about to exit the oak grove and enter the parking area, Gordon held up his hand and said, "I guess I was wrong. Look at the bottom of the door; there appear to be lights on in the facility. You can see it at the bottom. There must be activity going on inside. I don't think access is possible tonight. We better go quietly back and leave," said Gordon.

"Hold on," said Marcus. "I'd sure like to get a better look at that pallet in front of the main access door. It looked like it was loaded with fertilizer bags when we filmed it with the drone yesterday. That would make no sense for a bottling facility. No one appears to be outside. Maybe we can get up close and take a quick look before we leave."

Instead of answering, Gordon held up his hand, motioning for Marcus to stay put as he quickly moved towards the pallet. He had almost reached it when the main door of the facility started to slide open and the lights from inside began to flood the parking lot. The brightness instantly blinded Marcus with his night vision goggles on. Quickly removing them, he whispered, "Oh, shit."

As his vision cleared, he sensed possible panic. There were two men moving the pallet into the facility but no sign of Gordon. *They couldn't have caught Gordon and brought him inside in that short period of time when I was blinded. Where did he go?* wondered Marcus.

The pallet was moved inside slowly by two staff members and the facility door came down, shutting out all light in the parking area. *That's odd,* thought Marcus. *They appear to be taking extreme care in moving a pallet that only has fertilizer bags on it.*

Putting the night vision goggles back on, Marcus strained to see any sign of motion in the area where he thought Gordon should be. He was totally unaware of anyone coming up behind and jumped with fright as Gordon said softly, "Come, we best quickly leave as we came."

"Gordon, where did you come from? I thought they caught you up by the pallet."

"No, not at all. When I heard the motor start and the door just beginning to lift, I quickly scurried back into the oak grove and circled back here — but not empty-handed. While there, I cut a hole in one of the bags and scooped some of its contents into the pocket of my jacket. By the way, I don't think it's fertilizer. It has no odor at all and has an extremely fine consistency for fertilizer. It's almost like a powder. We can analyze it back at the house."

Marcus, taking one last look at the building as they were about to turn and leave, said, "We could have a problem. Look at the corner of the roof, Gordon. That could be a security camera up there. If it has infrared capability, we may be on film."

"Hopefully, with what we are wearing and with the night vision googles on we are not recognizable, but they will know someone was here."

They made their way back to their Vespas on the darkened road, unscathed but a little concerned with what the future could be.

Giovanni Toscano sat in his office contemplating his daughter's encounter with the tour guides from Tuscany Tours. *It is a bit unusual for them to be on that back road,* he thought. *But Natalie's inquiry to Tuscany Tours validated they worked there. The crop surveillance drone showed them returning the way they came after fixing her bike. If she sees them tonight at the festival, maybe we will learn more.*

I still think a call to my cousin in Venice might be worthwhile.

With that thought in mind, Giovanni reached down in the file drawer of his desk looking for the contact list that was generated at the family reunion five years before. *I have to admit, I never realized I had that many relatives,* he thought as he thumbed through the list looking for the cousin. "Here he is," he said out loud to himself and reading the entry, he said, "Salvatore Toscano - Agent, Italian Anti-Mafia Investigation Department. *Aw, oh, when I spoke to him all he said was he worked for the government on international crime. He didn't say anything about the Mafia. I better be careful how I verbalize my inquiry as to whether he is aware of any activity going on concerning Tuscan wineries and could the tour guides be investigators. It would not go well for him to find out what we are doing here. Maybe I'll wait and see what Natalie finds out at the festival.*

It was fairly late by the time Marcus and Gordon got back to the B&B. They were somewhat surprised not to find Abigail, Leo, and Martina at home. Gordon sensed the concern on Marcus's face and commented, "Marcus, not to worry. I'm sure Abigail is drinking wine with her friends and Leo and Martina are probably dancing away. The orchestra that they have usually plays until the last couple goes off the square."

Stowing the motor scooters, they went into the kitchen and Marcus watched with interest as Gordon emptied his jacket pocket of the powder he had taken from the bags at the winery. He proceeded to take quantities of the powder through several steps. Some involved heating it; others involved adding different solutions like bleach.

"Gordon, where did you learn all this? What are you testing for?" asked Marcus.

"I was part of the drug division in MI6 back in the UK. It was not uncommon for dogs to sniff out a potential smuggler at the airport. Upon confiscation of his luggage, we would do different tests to determine what he had. That's what I'm doing now. I can tell you for sure it's definitely cocaine, but I can't quite determine what they cut it with. Whatever it is, it changes its color and quite possibly mitigates the odor that drug dogs can sense."

"That answers one question that we had. We now know how cocaine is getting into the country. This could be a bear to discover at a port of entry. It could come in any container and the dogs would never find it," said Marcus.

"It also pretty much validates your original theory," responded Gordon. "If it's here at the winery in this form and being brought into the bottling facility as we observed, I think we can assume it's being processed into the wine for shipment as you suspected."

Then with a big smile he continued, "I think your job is pretty much done. Report this to the Italian authorities and they will take it from here. You and Leo can go back on home. Concerning the other issue that you're dealing with, it might not be a bad idea. Back in the UK or at home in the US, you may not have a Mafia price on your head."

"You could be right, but I think I'll wait until Leo and Martina get back before I call Agent Toscano."

Just then, they were both startled as Abigail rushed in, yelling loudly, "Oh no, they're not here." She was disheveled and had a frantic look on her face.

Gordon quickly said, "Abigail, what happened? What do you mean?"

"When I went looking for them at the piazza, they were not there. I went back to where we parked the bikes and both of theirs were gone. I just assumed they decided to go home by themselves."

"They wouldn't do that," said Marcus.

"Abigail, calm yourself," said Gordon. "Go through what happened slowly." Abigail related the whole evening: when they got there, who they saw, and when she sent them down to the piazza to dance.

"Do you think they tried to come home by themselves and got lost?" asked Gordon.

"I doubt that," said Marcus.

"Well, I know the area quite well. I'll take a Vespa and scout around. If they show up, call me." Before anyone could question him, Gordon was out the door.

"If they were kidnapped, I can't believe they would take their bikes too," said Abigail.

"You may be right, but I think I better I make a call," said Marcus as he pulled out his cell phone and tapped in a number. It was answered immediately and he said, "Brady. Thank God, you're back from your mission. We've got a problem."

In the dark of night the rig pulling the cargo container rumbled along the unimproved back road of Libbiano. It suddenly hit a pothole which caused the whole vehicle to bounce from the road jarring the cargo within the container. Dreaming, Leo with arms entwined around Martina cruised across the floor dancing cheek to cheek. The jar brought him into consciousness and then he realized that he was cheek to cheek with Martina, but constrained. He sensed the zip ties on his wrists and ankles and felt Martina's legs wrapped around him.

First whispering, then calling in a louder voice, he said, "Martina, Martina, wake up."

Her initial response was a groan followed by a cough, and then she said, "Leo, ow. I'm tied around you. What happened? Just then the rig hit another road rut and the two entwined bodies rolled. "Ow," cried Martina. "What's going on? It's so dark. I can't see anything but I feel zip ties on my wrists and ankles.

"We were drugged, and obviously have been captured by someone. Further, they appear to be a little sadistic. They have constrained us in the missionary position. I believe we are in a shipping container being taken somewhere." Just then the rig hit another large pothole.

Gordon stormed into the B&B, face covered with dust and said, "Marcus, are you armed? I think I have been followed. I covered the entire neighborhood. No sign of Martina and Leo. When I pulled onto our road, I picked up a follower. It was a car but it appeared to stay back, not overtaking me. If they were truly following me, they could be pulling into our place momentarily."

Marcus pulled out the Beretta that Martina had given him. There was a pounding on the door and Gordon went to it while Marcus stood back. Looking through the peephole, he quickly relaxed and began to open the door, saying over his shoulder, "Not to worry, Marcus. It's Agent Nelson."

As the door opened, Marcus called out, "Brady, I'm so glad you are here. We've lost Martina and Leo."

Abigail related her story of how they had gone into town to the festival and how they had disappeared when she went to look for them to go home. She explained that she discovered that their bikes were missing when she went to get her own. Gordon added that thinking they may have gotten lost, he had searched the entire neighborhood to no avail.

Brady listened to their stories and finally said, "It's the local Mafia. That's their MO. They make people disappear. They strive for the appearance that they were never here to begin with. That's why the bikes are gone too. It's commonly known that local police are part of the organization. I'm sure they were not too pleased with what Martina said and did to them the other day. They surely were part of the abduction. They probably were watching for her at the festival. They would know she came by bicycle. I have no idea where they would take them."

"Or if they are still alive," said Marcus in a slightly shaken voice.

Natalie rushed into her father's office when she returned to the winery. She knew he would want a report of how things went at the festival and if her bike-repair tour guides showed up. "Father, Father, you wouldn't believe!" She said as she entered his office, appearing upset. "Two of the tour guides did show up at our booth. The woman, and one of the men. We chatted and I gave them brochures. Much later, however, when we were closing down and I was loading our truck, down the road a ways, I spotted four men, two of them local police, loading what appeared to be the unconscious bodies of the tour guides. They were putting them into a van. They looked my way but I continued to load the truck, trying to appear that I was totally involved with loading and wasn't aware of their actions. They paid me no further attention and quickly drove off."

"Natalie, good move. Now go to bed and get some rest. I'll make some calls. This could be a local Mafia operation and it's good you didn't get involved. I have no idea why the tour guides would be abducted, but we will find out."

"Ow!" screamed Leo.

"Ow also," said Martina. "That last bump and us rolling really hurt. Are you okay, Leo?"

"Yes, but I think we rolled into something. It could be our bikes. I'm trying to wiggle my fingers and my hand around what we rolled into." There was a slight pause and then Leo said, "I think I got a wheel, a tire. I can feel the spokes. Martina, let's try to roll a little more in the same direction. If I can get close to the wheel and maybe the fender, I might be able to use it like a knife and move my wrists back and forth to cut the cable tie."

As Leo worked his wrists' cable ties back and forth on the fender, Martina chatted away, "Leo. I think I know who did this. When we were dancing, I spotted those two police that picked me up the other day. They were in the crowd mingling around the booths that surrounded the piazza. They could've recognized us and figured it was time to get even."

Leo didn't respond but just kept moving his wrists back and forth. In a somewhat lighter voice Martina continued, "It was nice of them to bring our bikes. If we figure out how to escape, we've got transportation."

Just then she was surprised as the arms around her came free and two hands grabbed her head, turned it slightly and she received a passionate kiss.

"I'm free," said Leo. "If I can get in my pocket, and it's still there, I have a small pocket knife."

The rig sped along the deserted Tuscan road, headlights piercing the darkness. Rounding a curve, the driver screamed out "NO" as the forms of two deer (a protected wildlife in Tuscany) crossing the road became visible. Immediately applying the brakes and swerving to miss them, the driver threw the rig into a crashing mode. The tractor went into a road-bordering tree, causing the driver and companion to go headlong into the windshield. Typical of their laxity, they weren't wearing their seatbelts. The tractor's diesel engine stalled and the container they were towing flipped over on its side. Screams could be heard as its contents tumbled. Then there was total quiet.

"Martina, are you okay," called Leo.

"Yes, but I think I might have a gash in my leg. I landed on one of the bicycles. It's lucky you got us loose before this happened. I don't know how we would have landed if we were still tied together," said Martina.

"Our bikes had headlights on them. One of them is bound to work," said Leo as he crawled around in the dark container. Finding the handlebars of one of the bicycles he turned on its light and twisted it out of its clamp. "At last we can see where we are," he said. "Wow, it's just us and our bicycles in this huge shipping container." Then looking at Martina, he said, "That's a pretty bad gash. We better tie something around it. I believe we were in a pretty bad accident. I'm not sure our captors survived. We have to get out of here if we can."

Ripping the sleeve off his shirt, Leo crawled over to Martina, saying, "Let me tie this on your wound. It should help stop the bleeding and protect it until we can get something better. Here, you hold the light while I work on your leg."

Suddenly the complete silence was broken by the sound of an owl hooting and a cool breeze floated over Martina and Leo. Martina quickly swung the light in the direction of the sound and breeze, saying, "Leo, I think we're free. It appears the rear closure of the container burst open when it flipped on its side."

"You are right," responded Leo. "It's so dark out we didn't notice it before. It probably wasn't locked as they thought we were tied up so no need to lock us in. The shock of the crash and the container going on its side caused the latches to open. Let's get out and away from here. Will you be able to walk or ride your bike if we can get them out of the container?"

"I'm sure. It's just a superficial scrape. It looks worse than it really is," said Martina.

Leo and Martina were surprised to find out that, though they had been drugged, tied up, and taken away, they had not been searched. They both still had all that they had on them before. This included their cell phones, which of course were dead and needed to be charged. And very surprisingly, Martina still had her Walther PPK in her shoulder holster. Obviously, inept captors.

While Leo had unloaded their bikes, Martina had checked the bodies of the driver and accomplice and found both to have no pulse. They were now riding in the opposite direction on the road that the rig had been traveling, assuming that was where they had come from. Their conversation had ceased and both rode in total silence, deep in their respective thoughts.

This has certainly been a harrowing experience, but dancing with Martina and waking up tied together wasn't all that bad. Then taking care of the gash in her leg. I don't know. I think I'm having feelings for her, thought Leo.

I know my primary objective was to get involved with Marcus, but I have to admit, Leo is beginning to turn my head, thought Martina.

As they came around a slight turn in the road, Martina said, "Oh look, it's beginning to get light. We must be going east."

"I believe we are on the road to Livorno," said Leo. "I bet they were going to load our container on some ship there, to get rid of us. That wouldn't have been a pleasant voyage."

"That's for sure," said Martina, "but it would have been a typical Mafia operation; we would have just disappeared."

"Look, there is a farm house up ahead and there are some lights on. Someone is up early," said Leo.

"They probably have cows to be milked. Let's stop and see if we can get some help. This gash is beginning to bleed again and they probably have a phone we can use."

They had no sooner pulled off onto the long driveway leading to the farmhouse when they heard the horrible sound of an Italian Emergency vehicle siren piercing the morning quiet. Looking back, they saw it speed by the driveway in the direction they had come.

"Either one of our captors was still alive and, regaining consciousness, called for help or someone else discovered the wreck. If it was the former, we could still be in danger," said Leo.

"I don't know, Leo. When I checked them, there was definitely no breathing, and checking for a pulse, I got no sense of a heartbeat. I'm sure they were dead."

"At this stage of things, I don't think we can be sure of anything," said Leo.

"We better be cool when we meet the farmhouse family. Let's just say you hit a rock in the road that you didn't see in the dark and going down you got the gash in your leg. Careful now, there appear to be some dogs coming out to greet us. With any luck, their master will appear and call them off as we get close."

Marcus had gotten no sleep at all. Before he left, Brady Nelson had put out an APB to his contacts and told Marcus and the Smyths to go to bed as there was nothing else they could do till morning. It was just beginning to get light as Marcus struggled into the kitchen and was surprised to see Abigail there making coffee.

"It's my treat," she said as Marcus entered the kitchen. "Gorden is typical English and must have his tea in the morning but I like my coffee. Want some?"

"Oh, please," said Marcus. "I didn't get much sleep at all last night but I still need something to clear my head. I don't know what we do. They could be held captive somewhere or they could be dead. You can't call the local police as they are part of the local Mafia and Agent Toscano is in Venice. I am totally frustrated."

Just then the Smyth phone rang.

CHAPTER 10

Escape from Tuscany

T he loud ringing of the phone startled Marcus and he almost choked on the hot coffee he was drinking. He carefully set the cup down on the kitchen table while exhibiting an anticipatory gaze at Abigail as she crossed the room and picked up the phone.

"Hello. Oh, Martina, are you okay? Where are you?"

"Thank God. Okay, I'll hang up and we will wait. That was Martina. They are okay and they are at a farmhouse somewhere outside of Livorno. She said there's lots to tell but they don't want to impose on the residents. They are charging their cell phones and will call on them just as soon as they can," said Abigail.

"I'll call Brady to let him know the status but until they call back, there is not much we can do," said Marcus. Just then Gordon entered the room and they both brought him up to speed.

Agent Toscano sat at his desk in Venice somewhat perplexed. It had been days since he had heard directly from either Agent Peterson or Agent Harris. The last word was that they were settled in a safe house run by a retired MI6 agent outside of San Gimignano and were planning a closer surveillance of the Tuscano winery.

The thought that a winery run by a distant relative was involved with the Mafia and internationally dealing in drugs did not sit well with him. Further, having two young MI6 and CIA agents assigned to his office for international experience now possibly in a murderous environment also gave him concern. His thought process was interrupted by his secretary as she burst into his office saying, "Sir, we just intercepted a rumble on the net that a local Mafia family in Tuscany are claiming to have abducted and accomplished the demise of an MI6 agent and an Italian Interpol agent. This supposedly is in retribution for an incident occurring in San Gimignano. This is not going over well with the *capo di tutti*. Evidently the Sicilian Mafia have an operation going on there that they do not want discovered by government law enforcement."

"Thank you, Silvia. Get me Agent Romano on the phone. This is not good. Internal Mafia squabbles are bad enough; involving murderous events concerning government law enforcement is a crisis issue. Quickly, please, Silvia." *I'm sure it's Agent Harris and Agent Bufalino who are involved,* thought Agent Toscano. *And when we investigate, no one will have seen or heard anything. These are the times I hate this job.*

Ten kilometers outside of San Gimignano on the road to Livorno, a vacant San Gimignano police car was discovered by a local farmer. He was driving his produce into town to market. Surprised to see the doors open and no indication of anyone around, he stopped to investigate. The vehicle had been totally stripped of its contents, its radio ripped from the dashboard and any firearms that might have existed were gone. Concerned, he called the local emergency number on his cell phone.

Giovanni was concerned with what Natalie told him occurred at the festival. This immediately put into question the real identity of the so-called tour guides. He had a good relationship with the local Mafia in that they didn't bother him and he ignored their existence. He was quite sure that they had no idea of the Sicilian Mafia operation going on at the winery. Walking into his office, he was surprised to see the message button lit on the phone. Picking up the receiver, he pressed the button and listened.

"Giovanni, Luciano here. You will be receiving two packages today that I wish placed in the current container going to the US with infused wine. When they are loaded, text me a picture of them. I will be forwarding it to your local family Don. *Grazie.*"

I don't know what Luciano is up to, he thought, *but the last thing I need is involvement in an inter-family squabble.*

Though it had only been a matter of days, Jenna felt it was an eternity since she had returned to New York and hadn't heard any word from either Agent Nelson or Marcus. It was Saturday morning and she came into the office to catch up on the background investigations that she had been assigned. Trying to stay focused, she decided another call to her friend in the FBI might be in order. Most all the other cubicles in her part of the office were empty, so she felt a cell phone call could safely be accomplished. Speaking on her cell phone, she said, "Hi Fred, sorry to bother you on the weekend. I don't have anything officially for you, but I had an inquisitive thought. I believe generally you try to keep tabs on what legitimate businesses the five local Mafia families are involved in. I know years ago they ran speakeasies during prohibition and illegally were peddling booze. Today, are you aware of any of the families operating legitimate liquor and wine stores? Specifically, possibly the Gambioni family. I remember from my last assignment, Angelina loved her wine."

Just then she was startled as the PA system boomed. "Jenna, Security told me you are in. Come to my office, please."

"Sorry about that, Fred. Have to run. My boss likes to use the PA system instead of a phone. If you find out anything, get back to me. I might have something for you." Slipping her cell phone back in her pocketbook on her desk, she hustled off to her boss's office.

When she entered, he motioned her to sit and said, "Jenna, I just received a classified report from MI6 in the UK. It's actually a copy of a report that Marcus and Agent Harris filed today from Italy. It appears that cockamamie story you told me when you came home from your little vacation is true. They have confirmed that the Toscano winery in Tuscany is infusing cocaine in their wine and exporting it via container ship. Where has not been determined. Oh, also it seems that Agent Harris and Martina Bufalino were abducted by the local Mafia in San Gimignano but escaped. No details on their whereabouts or Marcus's."

"Are they OK? No other details?"

"No. I'm sure we would have heard from Agent Nelson if there were any issues. Even though he is on another assignment there, he is keeping an eye on their activities."

Seeing the distraught look on her face, he continued, "Don't be concerned, Jenna. I'm sure Marcus is fine. You shouldn't be in here today anyway. Those background investigations you are working on don't need to be done on overtime. Go home. Enjoy the rest of your weekend."

Easy for you to say, thought Jenna as she left his office.

The morning sun spilling over the front porch of the farm house provided a very warm environment for Leo and Martina. Both were on their cell phones, Martina sitting on the porch swing and speaking to Abigail while Leo sat at the other end of the porch in a wicker chair speaking to Marcus. Both finished their conversations and began speaking almost simultaneously.

Martina said, "Abigail says it will be at least two to three hours before Gordon can get to us. He has to borrow a truck from a neighbor to be able to carry the bikes back with us."

Leo said, "Marcus says that Brady told him we should stay away from the winery. There is an internal Mafia family dispute going on and we should try not to get involved though we are the probable cause."

"Okay, you first, Martina," said Leo and Martina restated the Abigail message. "Well, that means we're here for a while. By the way, I'm having difficulty understanding the farmer and his wife."

"I'm not surprised. They speak a slightly different Italian dialect. I'm used to it, as my mother spoke that same dialect. It's not Roman and it's not Sicilian — it's something in between. By the way, she looked at my gash and she is getting some antibiotic salve and a bandage for me. She told me that being so remote they have to keep medical supplies on hand just in case one of them gets hurt doing the normal chores at a farm.

"Look, if we get my gash cleaned up and bandaged, I'm sure I can ride my bike. We don't really have to stay here. It's a single road back toward San Gimignano. We could meet Gordon on the way."

Just then the screen door opened and the farmer's wife arrived with the meds for the gash, coffee, and a basket of *biscotti*. Eying the food, Leo said with a slight smile, "I guess it would be impolite to rush off." Neither was aware that the farmer was inside, busy on his phone.

As Abigail hung up her phone and Marcus put his cell phone away, Gordon rushed into the kitchen and looking at Marcus, said, "It's good you three live out of your suitcases. It was easy for me to pack. Marcus, one thing we've learned living here, you trust no one unless you know them. I have packed your suitcases and put them in the Maserati while you were on the phone. I have programed the GPS to the farmhouse they are staying at. Go pick them up and go straight to Rome. That's Martina's home base so you should be safe there. I will call Brady and let him know the plan.

"You should be able to reach the farmhouse in less than an hour, with luck, before any other unwanted visitors approach. Quickly, go now."

In a matter of minutes goodbyes and thank you's were exchanged and Marcus was speeding towards Livorno in the Maserati.

◍

Agent Toscano was relieved and somewhat excited as he got off the phone with Brady Nelson.

I have to admit I'm never thrilled having the CIA operating in my country, thought Agent Toscano, *but there are times, like now, when they can be an asset.*

"Sylvia, get Romano back on the phone, please," he called out while thinking, *It's time to get 'Operation Vineyard' rolling. We have enough evidence to make a raid and the quicker the better.*

Picking up the receiver of the buzzing phone on his desk, he said, "Romano, it's time. But I want you to lead the raid. I can't be involved. It's a family matter; just leave it at that. Our visiting agents are supposedly on their way to the Interpol offices in Rome. I will travel down there to debrief them and send them back to the UK. You can conduct the raid as early as tomorrow."

"Not a problem," responded Agent Romano. "I have been assembling a task force in San Gimignano since the winery came under suspicion."

◍

Martina was in deep conversation with the farmer's wife and Leo was dipping his third *biscotto* in his coffee when his cell phone rang. "Leo here."

Martina stopped her chat and looked over at Leo as he answered the phone. He appeared to have a serious concentrated look on his face and then she heard him say, "I understand. Will do. Yes, we will be ready. Thanks." And he hung up.

"What was that all about?" she asked.

"Oh, nothing major. Just a status on our pickup," He said with a slight smile and picked up his third *biscotto*.

◍

The pickup was executed perfectly. The farmer's wife couldn't believe what she was witnessing. The sports car zoomed down her driveway and came to a screeching stop in front of her porch and her two guests were off the porch and in the car in a matter of seconds. Then it zoomed away.

"Great driving," said Leo. "What's up?"

"Just a cautionary move," responded Marcus, "suggested by Gordon."

Then looking in the rearview mirror and seeing a black Daimler-Benz going into the driveway, he continued with, "From what I see in the rearview mirror, it appears it was a wise move. Someone just drove into the driveway we left. It could be unwanted visitors looking for us. Luckily, we were well on our way before they came around that curve in the road prior to the farm house driveway.

Oh, I forgot to tell you we're not going back to the Smyth's. We are on our way to Rome."

"What!" screamed Martina. "My clothes!"

"Don't panic," responded Marcus. "We are all packed and our bags are in the trunk. We turn off this road and go south just a short distance from here, I hope before our unwanted visitors come looking for us. If we are lucky, they will think we are going back towards San Gimignano and will be off our trail.

Giovanni sat at his desk contemplating the phone message he had received from Luciano. The drug operation he was accomplishing for the Sicilian family was quite lucrative and being at odds with any organized crime family could be deadly. *What to do?* he thought.

Just then the interoffice phone on his desk rang and picking it up, he heard a frazzled voice saying, "Salvatori here at the fusing facility. A pickup truck just drove in, rolled two bodies out on the ground and drove off. By the uniforms they are wearing, they appear to be local police. They are bound up with zip ties and have tape over their mouths. They appear to be drugged."

"See if you can bring them around. I'm going to make a call but I'll be right down," said Giovanni. Then picking up his outside phone, he dialed Luciano Guerra.

"Luciano, what are you requesting? Murder is not in our operating plan. This is not good."

"Not to worry, Giovanni. Just do as I say. I've made arrangements in Livorno. They will be released from the container before it is loaded on a ship. I'm just sending a message to your local Mafia family. You don't mess with Sicilian Mafiosi."

⊕

They had been traveling no more than 15 minutes, Marcus shifting up and down as they drove the winding roads through the Tuscan hillsides. During this time, Leo monopolized the conversation, describing to Marcus what he and Martina had endured when kidnapped. This entire time, Martina said nothing, just staring ahead and appearing to be in another world. Leo had just finished describing what had happened at the farmhouse when Martina startled both he and Marcus by saying in a somewhat stern voice, "There is space coming up on the road on our side. Pull over, please. I'm driving."

"What's going on? What's the matter?" asked Marcus.

"Look, Gordon's idea was good. We definitely had to make a run for it. But going to Rome only provides safety for us. It doesn't help with the case at hand. We know what's going on in the winery. We don't know where it's going or where it's coming from. All we know is containers are coming and leaving the winery and Italy via Livorno. We must go there to continue our investigation. I know the roads here, Marcus. The next major town we will be hitting is Siena, and just prior to entering that town there is a side road that will bring us back to the coast. There we can travel back up to Livorno. I know you're having fun driving this Maserati but it's my turn now."

Begrudgingly, Marcus pulled off the road and they exchanged drivers. Martina had barely pulled back on the road when Marcus said in a somewhat doubtful voice, "How are we going to find out where the shipping container from the winery is or where it's going? You see them stacked up in the port. There is absolutely no way we will be able to find or identify the one from the winery, Martina. This is going to be a worthless trip."

"Marcus, you are so wrong. This actually will be the easiest part of our investigation," responded Martina. "Welcome to the investigative capability of Interpol. Needless to say, this is one of the areas that I've been schooled in. When we get to Livorno, I will be taking you to Central Port Control and there you will be amazed.

"If you ever took notice, every shipping container has a BL number stenciled on the side. Further, in today's world most all containers have a tracking device either mounted internally or externally. It's about the size of a deck of cards so it's not very noticeable. However, when that container enters the port facility gate, it's photographed and its tracking device signal is picked up. They know where it came from and they know where it will be placed in the port and ultimately they'll know what ship it was put on. They will also know what it is supposed to contain in that its cargo must be declared when it is scheduled to be shipped. You have to understand, time is critical to the logistics of the world. Some shipping companies like Mersk own their containers and provide them to the shipper when contracted for product shipment. Alternately, a company may own their own or rent them, delivering them to a shipping company themselves. In either case, all want to know where their product is at any time and when will it arrive at its ultimate destination. Luckily, in our high tech world today we have that capability.

"It's not clear what concept the Toscano winery is using as the one container we saw had no external markings other than its BL number. Further, if you recall, we saw the cocaine in bags marked as fertilizer on a skid. We don't know whether that skid came in the container that was there, or had arrived earlier and we didn't actually see them loading wine into the container. We obviously know who is shipping the wine and we suspect we know who is shipping the cocaine, as we saw Carlos Calisto at the wine tasting. Most likely, we will learn more in Livorno."

⏀

All was quiet in the Maserati as they sped along to Livorno. Marcus's head was abuzz with thoughts. *This certainly has been a wild assignment,* he thought. *I have been seeing parts of Italy I have only dreamed about. I have killed a man, and even though it was justified as it was in self-defense, I still took another person's life. I'm not really sure how I deal with that. If I stay in this profession, that might only be the beginning. I had a liaison with Martina who I thought I could be attracted to but now I'm not so sure. And the brief visit with Jenna put that further into question. Despite my protective associates, local organized crime is trying to assassinate me. Is this what they consider operational training?*

"Marcus. Marcus, are you sleeping? Wake up," said Martina.

"No, no, I'm not sleeping, just mentally reviewing our activities. What's up?"

"We're coming into Livorno. Set up Tuscany Tours on the GPS. I put it in there earlier. We will stop there first.

"Leo! See if you can get Sophia on your cell phone. You should have a local service now. Tell her we're coming and we might need a place to stay and possibly a car to borrow. I don't think the Maserati is the car to be driving into the port area."

Jenna, sitting at home, just wasn't able to get Marcus out of her head and she had finally gotten to the point where she thought she would try to call his cell, even knowing that was basically forbidden. "One never initiates a call to an agent in the field unless it is scheduled as one never knows the operational status of the agent and an incoming call could be compromising to his situation." She had just picked up her phone and was about to dial when it rang.

"Jenna here," she said. "Oh hi, Fred, thanks for the return call. Did you learn anything?"

"I hope your meeting with your boss went all right," said Fred. "Since you didn't call back, I proceeded to investigate. Surprisingly, your questioning thoughts were right. A member of the Gambioni family has opened a wine and spirits shop. It's not under the Gambioni name, but our sources tell us it's part of that Mafia family. However, it wouldn't be considered unusual as most of the families have legitimate businesses and their racketeering activities are carried out behind the scenes. I thought you were working on cocaine coming into the country. What does that have to do with wine?"

"You will you be getting a detail report shortly from the CIA but let me fill you in on what we know," replied Jenna.

⊕

The Maserati sped along SS1, the main freeway on the west coast of Italy, heading into Livorno. Leo chatted to Sophia on his cell phone. Martina, weaving through traffic and watching the off-ramp signs, said, "There are several off-ramps as we come into Livorno. See if you can determine on the GPS which one she will be taking us off on. I want to stay in the fast lane as long as possible but things could get dicey as traffic picks up and getting over to an exit in time could be a problem without enough warning."

As Marcus scanned the GPS, his cell phone rang. Leo quickly said goodbye to Sophia and told her he would call her back. Marcus struggled to get the phone out of his jacket pocket, then answered, "Hello, Agent Peterson here. Oh, Agent Toscano. No, we are not on our way to Rome; we are heading into Livorno." Then he said nothing.

Martina continued driving and Leo closed his phone and watched Marcus. He kept nodding his head and after several minutes said, "Yes, I understand. We will proceed."

Closing the phone, he announced, "As you heard, that was Agent Toscano. He has been trying to contact us for some time and didn't get through until we started coming into Livorno and picked up cell service. When I told him we were not on our way into Rome as instructed, he became quite upset. He immediately and correctly assumed that we were going to check on the shipping container. His instruction, more like a direct order, was to proceed to the local airport located between Livorno and Pisa, called the Pisa Galileo Galilei Airport."

"I know it well," said Martina. "Easy Jet and Ryanair operate out of there. I have flown there from Rome. If we stay on SS1 it will bring us right to it."

Marcus continued, "Agent Toscano went on to say we should not follow up on the shipping container issue and do not go near the port. We will be met at the rental car return at the airport and all will be explained. Seems there is another operation going on at the port and they wanted to avoid any possible interference."

Turning to face Leo in the back of the car and looking out the rear window, he said, "Oh, Martina, your driving skills I believe are about to be tested. Traffic is getting heavy but I think I see a black Daimler-Benz a ways behind us. If it's the one I saw going into the farmer's driveway after we left, we could be in for a problem. They probably got a description of our car from the farmer.

"Leo, you try and keep an eye on them. They are in the fast lane like we are and pretty far back. With this traffic and the Maserati being pretty low, it will be a little difficult. You will probably only see them when the road rises with the terrain.

"I'll get on the GPS and see what options we have going forward," continued Marcus.

All was quiet in the car as they sped along and traffic continued to grow as they came into Livorno proper. Then Marcus shouted out, "Martina, get over to the slow lane. The next exit appears to be a main road to the port. Leo, see if the Daimler-Benz moves over when we do. If it does, they are definitely following us."

Marcus went back to scanning the GPS, then said, "Martina, the GPS shows an on-ramp immediately following the off-ramp."

Martina replied, "Yes I see a road sign indicating the same; it's coming up in three clicks. When the exit comes up, let's get off and get right back on. Conceivably, with traffic permitting we will be off and back on before the Daimler-Benz catches up. If we're lucky, they will see us get off and not get back on and will think we went to the port."

While Marcus and his friends were busy playing cat and mouse on the SS1 freeway, Agent Toscano was on the phone busily organizing their airport greeting party. It appeared that serendipity was playing a role in events. The highly classified international arms deal being tracked by both the US and Italian investigative branches was about to culminate with a raid on the suspected perpetrators in Livorno. This had considerably higher priority than any drug-shipping operation. This was about to happen now, where follow-up on the drug shipment could be delayed. His hope was to contact either Italian Financial Guard Agent Rossi or US CIA Agent Brady Nelson who were in the Livorno area to meet Marcus, Leo, and Martina at the airport, explain the situation and send them on their way.

CHAPTER 11

Case Closed

All appeared to have gone well on the final drive to the airport. Apparently the black Benz did not get back on SS1, so must've assumed the Maserati was going to the port. With the afternoon traffic, it would probably be a while before they discovered their mistake.

Upon reaching the airport proper, they were able to turn in the Maserati at car rental and proceed to the departure area where they were told they would be met. Between the perimeter road and the terminal was a large grassy area sprinkled with trees and statuary. Adjacent to the departure entrance, a café had an outdoor seating area where the trio had been told to wait. The afternoon sun was still high, but their table was shaded by the café's partially-opened awning. Lattes and a tea had been ordered and served.

"Leo, is tea always a requirement?" asked Marcus.

"Marcus, at home, precisely at three, it's time for tea and biscuits. The biscuits are what you would normally call cookies and they may be served with double cream. I don't know whether you would call that a tradition or what, but that's just normally what happens. I guess if you're not English, you just wouldn't understand."

"Marcus, did Agent Toscano say who would be meeting us?" asked Martina.

How do I answer this? thought Marcus. *Toscano told me it would either be Rossi or Brady Nelson, but Brady had warned us that he preferred Martina to not know he was around or involved and so far, we have been able to maintain his desire. I'll have to just make it up.*

"No, not directly. He just said it would be one of the agents and that we'd recognize him." Just then their conversation was drowned out by the noise of the jet taking off, immediately followed by two pops like fireworks going off.

"I wonder what that was?" asked Marcus as he looked out towards the runway. Receiving no response, he looked back at Martina and Leo. Color drained from his face and he screamed as loud as he could, "Oh, no." Sitting opposite him were two lifeless bodies with quarter inch holes in their foreheads and blood trickling down from the back of their heads.

Brady Nelson was coming across the lawn and, seeing Marcus, he came running. By the time he reached the table, both bodies had fallen out of their chairs, exposing a huge gash in the back of each head. Marcus was just sitting there like a statue, color completely drained from his face, staring at where Leo and Martina had been sitting.

"Marcus," called Brady, and seeing no response, he slapped him on the face saying, "Marcus, snap out of it. Come with me. We can do nothing here. Authorities will take over. It was obviously a Mafia sniper." Looking down at the bodies he continued, "Damn, he used hollowpoint bullets. Blew the back of their heads wide open."

With tears appearing on Marcus's face, he cried out, "Why, why? They were my friends. Why?"

Brady grabbed Marcus's arm and his bag, hustling him through the crowd that was gathering and over to his car parked on the perimeter road. Speaking fast in a somewhat monotone voice, he said, "Quickly, Marcus, we must phase out of here. It would not be wise for US CIA agents to be involved in a local murder. You are lucky to be alive. The only thing that saved you was your back was obviously to the shooter and your hair is still dyed black. Mafia snipers quickly make their hit and leave. He recognized Leo and Martina, shot and left. Crime scene authorities will determine where he shot from and when they question those in that area, no one will have witnessed anything. This will go down as another unsolved murder. That appears to be just the way it is in this country.

Either your phone or Agent Toscano's must have been tapped as they knew you were coming here.

Quickly get in the car, we are going over to the civil side of the airport. There is a Gulfstream G 650 waiting for us. We all have been ordered home. Now it's just the two of us but as far as our agencies are concerned, our cases are closed."

As Brady rattled on and they sped around the perimeter road, Marcus had a blank stare on his face and softly said, "I still have the Beretta she gave me. Not sure our relationship would've gone anywhere but I really considered her a true friend. And Leo, who will tell MI6, and my clothes and stuff. Leo and I share an apartment in the UK. Somehow, I have to get there. Is this plane taking us to the UK or home?"

"Marcus. Marcus, did you hear a word I said?" yelled Brady as he parked his car on the flight line next to the Gulfstream. It had zero markings except for a tail number.

Its boarding ramp was down and a uniformed female flight attendant at the top called out,

"Where are the other two? We have a short window and must be leaving now. Commercial in and out will block us for several hours if we don't."

"They won't be coming," responded Brady. "As soon as we board, we can leave." Then turning to Marcus, he said, "We will discuss all this on board. Quick now, grab your bag."

The interior of the Gulfstream was quite lavishly appointed. Boarding was forward where there was seating for four around a table. This was followed with the lounge area with seating for another four and included a sideboard with a large TV. The seating was done in white leather with the other trim in mahogany. As they settled in their seats in the lounge area, all Marcus could say was, "Wow, is this a CIA plane?"

"Yes, but not to worry," responded Brady. "It wasn't paid for by taxpayer money. It was appropriated from a Mexican drug cartel bust. It gives us clandestine worldwide transportation capability, which is critical when an extraction is necessary, such as now. The flight attendant is actually a CIA agent. The uniform is for appearance at the airport. We want to appear as a business charter plane.

"Had you followed orders, it would have been waiting for you in Rome. It was still in flight when agent Toscano found out you were headed to Livorno. So he had it diverted. The original plan was to extract you and Leo from Rome. The Interpol agency in Rome would have taken care of Martina. I suspect that when the local Mafia found out you were headed to the Pisa airport, they immediately put their plan in operation, which was to take out Martina for what she had done to them and to take you out to collect the Gambioni bounty. Unfortunately for Leo, he was just with the wrong people at the wrong time. Luckily for you, the sniper didn't recognize you.

"Now to your original question. We are flying to the UK. That was part of the original plan to drop off Leo before taking you back to the US. We will lay over there 24 hours, which will allow you to collect your stuff from your shared apartment and provide a report to MI6. I would suggest you start preparing that report now as it is only a little over a two-hour flight to Gatwick and I'm sure MI6 will be meeting our flight."

CHAPTER 12

The Trip Home

Marcus sat busy at his laptop, typing away then stopping suddenly as he heard a strange sound coming from Brady. Looking over at him, he was shocked to see a man he had not seen before. His face was contorted and it looked as if he was about to cry.

"Brady, Brady, what's the matter? Are you alright? What is it?" he said.

Brady responded in a broken voice, "She was my daughter." Then he literally began to sob.

"Oh, no. How? Oh, my God," said Marcus as he went over and put his arm around him to try to comfort him.

Pulling his emotions together, Brady told Marcus about his affair with Martina's mother. He admitted she had never confirmed that Martina was his daughter but having and ending an affair with a married women does not lend itself to continual communication. Living in countries thousands of miles apart didn't help either. But it probably saved her marriage. Through the years she did keep him on the distribution of their family Christmas card, which allowed him to follow Martina's upbringing.

"Wow, you might have become my father-in-law," said Marcus.

"What do you mean?"

"Well, she really wanted to come to the US and on my last assignment she pretty much made a play for me even though Jenna and I were undercover as a married couple and pretty much acting the part. Now on this assignment she continued, but I think finally gave up when Jenna showed up in San Gimignano on the bus trip. I'll have to admit, she was one classy lady. I did think seriously about it. I believe Leo was really attracted to her and he could have become your son-in-law."

"Well, if that had happened, that is, if either of you married her, just maybe her mother would've told her and me, but we'll never know."

Due to weather, the flight to Gatwick was a little over three hours. As predicted, agents from MI6 met them and they proceeded to MI6 headquarters. It was a bit of an emotional meeting, as the staff and Leo's boss were extremely fond of Leo and his demise was difficult to accept. Marcus presented his full report and MI6 indicated they would be following up with the Italian Anti-Mafia Investigation Department. Further, MI6, aware of Marcus and Leo's living arrangements, told Marcus that they would handle contacting Leo's family and clearing the apartment of his things. They were both told to report back to Gatwick the following morning.

Brady had friends that he was going to visit and stay with while Marcus would proceed to the apartment he shared with Leo. His plan was to pack up all his clothes and gear to take back on the CIA Gulfstream and when finished, to possibly go to the old pub that he and Leo used to frequent.

As he packed his clothes, he was happy to think that shortly he would be home in his apartment having his complete wardrobe available and no longer living out of a suitcase. When he finished packing his clothes, he took his laptop out and set it up on the desk he used to use. When he and Leo had moved into the apartment, there was only one desk. They had flipped a coin and Marcus had won. Plugging in the phone line and logging in, he was happy to see they still had Internet capability. Luckily, they had paid their phone bill in advance prior to going to Italy. *With the six-hour time difference, Jenna should be at work. Maybe I can get a skype call in,* he thought.

Jenna responded immediately and they were face-to-face again. "Marcus, it's wonderful to see and hear you, but I'm so sorry, what a tragedy. I only briefly knew Leo but certainly knew Martina after we both spent 12 days with her on that cruise. What a loss. What a disaster."

Jenna's opening words triggered emotion in Marcus and there was a momentary pause before he could respond. "Yes, we were literally just hours away from being extracted to safety. It was horrible," said Marcus before he choked up again.

Seeing the emotion displayed on Marcus's face, Jenna quickly changed the subject, saying,

"Oh, Marcus, you will be happy to hear the FBI checked into the Gambioni family activity and as suspected, they have opened a wine shop that specializes in imported Italian wines. Further, the FBI was able to trace containers coming in from the Toscano winery and where they were delivered. They are planning a raid as we speak."

At those words, Marcus's face lit up but then went to a serious expression as he said, "Jenna, Franco may be in prison and Angelina is running the mob, but Franco put a price on my head in Italy and I'm convinced that was the main cause of Leo and Martina's demise. If I had been recognized by the sniper, we wouldn't be talking. As of now, I am initiating a vendetta against the Gambioni family."

"Marcus, stop," said Jenna. "You are not Italian or Mafia. You are a law-abiding US citizen. A CIA agent. Don't let your thoughts emulate the thoughts of those we track."

"I'm sorry, Jenna. Maybe the weeks I spent in Italy and the events that happened just turned my head. Further, I don't believe that explosion we experienced entering the condo that Franco wanted us to have was an accident. It was planned, executed, and caused extreme harm to the person I seriously care for. Somehow he is going to pay and I'm going to do everything I can to make sure that happens."

Marcus's words generated both warmth and fear in Jenna's head. *He obviously seriously cares for me, but his talk of vengeance scares me,* she thought.

It was the traditional happy hour in London when Marcus left the apartment and walked to the Old Swan pub on Kensington Church Street in Notting Hill, the place that he and Leo had frequented many times in the past. The sun had set and the streets were crowded with locals returning home from work. There was the usual crowd outside as well as in it.

"Marcus," called the bartender, as Marcus pushed his way to the bar. "We have missed you. You have been gone so long and where is your partner?"

"Oh, it's a sad story, Paddy," said Marcus. "He won't be joining me anymore, and I will be returning shortly to the US. We've been in Tuscany, Italy, these past weeks, and living on wine. Please pour me a pint to clear my throat and I will tell you the story."

Securing a seat at the end of the bar and devouring two pints of ale, Marcus was able to relate an abridged version of the escapade he and Leo had experienced in Italy. It ended with him describing the accidental death of his partner, not revealing the real details. There was a bit of a tear in both their eyes as he finished his story and then Paddy placed a plate of fish and chips in front of him: Marcus's favorite dinner, Old Swan's version of fish and chips, with chips, mushy peas, and beer-battered cod, with both tartar and curry sauces.

"Eat and drink, my friend. It's on the house. We will miss you both," he said.

It was fairly late when Marcus got back to the apartment but only four o'clock in the afternoon in New York. He felt another skype call to Jenna was definitely in order. She would be fast asleep in the morning when he would be taking off from Gatwick. The time at the pub had been good. The camaraderie of the staff, especially Paddy the bartender, helped ease the pain of losing Leo, but now Marcus's thoughts were only of Jenna and being home with her.

He fired up his laptop one more time and Jenna quickly answered the skype call. "Marcus, it's great to hear and see you again. What's up?" Then, seeing the emotion on Marcus's face, she asked, "Marcus, what's the matter? Are you okay?"

"I'm fine, Jenna. Right now I just miss you so terribly much. I wish I could be holding you in my arms. You will be fast asleep when we take off in the morning so I felt another call was in order. I really have strong feelings for you, Jenna. They really surfaced during the last 48 hours. Though I was dealing with the tragedy of the loss of our friends, deep down I was thinking of you and realizing I never want to lose you."

Jenna's face lit up like a neon sign. With sparkling eyes and a huge smile, she said, "Oh Marcus, you won't. It's only a matter of hours and we will be together. I've been told that you will be landing at LaGuardia and I have been assigned to meet the plane. Since you will be arriving in early afternoon, they want both you and Brady to report to the office. I will have a car to take you. There will also be an SUV there to transport your luggage to wherever you want it to go. Now get to bed and get some rest. See you soon. I love you. Bye," she said and her image was gone.

It was still dark when Marcus's cell phone rang. Grabbing it off the table, he said, "Hello. Oh Brady, hello. What time is it? It's still dark. Six o'clock. My alarm must not have gone off. Glad you called. You can come by and pick me up? That'll be great. I can be ready to go by eight, no problem.

"Hold on. Somebody just entered the apartment. I can tell because of the system Leo and I set up. Out of habit I must've turned it on last night when I came home. If the system is on, when the front door opens it lights a small red light we have in both bedrooms. We set it up when we moved in. The red light is on so someone definitely just came into the apartment."

Putting the cell phone on speaker and back down on the table, Marcus picked up his Beretta, which was under his pillow. He had made a habit of sleeping with it ever since Martina gave it to him. *Whoever came in will probably go in Leo's room first before coming down the hall to mine,* he thought. *And whoever they are, they must be wearing night vision goggles because they haven't turned on the lights.*

Marcus slowly opened his bedroom door. *If I turn on the lights, I should momentarily blind whoever came in, enabling me to accost him before he attacks me,* thought Marcus. In a quick move, he stepped into the hall, hit the light switch and crouched to the floor. At that instant, whoever was standing at the other end of the hall fired a shot that went wild, hitting a picture on the wall at the end of the hall. He was a tall individual, totally dressed in black and he held an unidentifiable pistol in his hand.

Marcus felt he had no choice. He fired four shots from his Beretta and the assailant went down.

Approaching the body to assure that it was incapacitated, he found that three shots had hit in the chest and one directly between the eyes. The assailant was dead.

He then became conscious of the voice coming from his cell phone. "Marcus. Marcus, what happened?" said Brady.

Marcus went back in the bedroom, quickly picking up the phone, and explained to Brady what had just occurred. Still on speaker, Brady said, "Get dressed, get your things, get out of the apartment. Go at least a block away and call and tell me where you are. I'll come pick you up."

This will be a second time I've left a dead body in a country I was in, thought Marcus as he said over the phone, "Will do. The Hubbub Bar and Kitchen is a block and a half away. We used to go there for breakfast. It's on West Ferry Road; you can't miss it. I'm on my way," and hung up the phone.

Marcus had just got his coffee and settled on an outside table when a white van pulled up and Brady jumped out. Running to the back of the van and opening the doors, he called to Marcus, "Quick, Marcus. Bring your gear."

In a matter of minutes, they loaded Marcus's gear in the back of the van and both were seated in the front with the driver. "To the civil side of Gatwick, please. The charter plane area. There is a Gulfstream waiting for us," said Brady to the driver, then turning to Marcus, he said, "You are a lucky pup sitting out in the open like that. You were an easy target for a sniper. I'm sure it was a follow-up hit by the Italian Mafia. They probably searched Leo's body after we left Pisa and found his driver's license and apartment keys, then sent someone over to make the hit. They want that bounty. It's all over for them once you get back to the states.

"It may be a while before they know the hit at the apartment failed and they start looking for you. I called MI6 as soon as I hung up from you. They said they would try to get to the apartment before the locals did as well as send a van to pick me up and now you. If all goes to plan, we get to Gatwick undetected."

Due to the early morning hour, the drive to the airport went faster than normal and it was also uneventful. The Mafia must not yet have discovered their hit failed and/or they had no idea where Marcus had gone. Commercial airline traffic was light, allowing the CIA Cessna an almost immediate takeoff slot. Brady and Marcus settled in for a very relaxing but also productive six- hour flight home. The CIA staffer that doubled as a flight attendant served up a very luxurious brunch that included champagne and American coffee.

Marcus settled down with his laptop and Brady logged onto the onboard PC. Both knew a report of their activities would be required upon checking in. After a while the silence of the cabin was broken when out of the blue, Brady said, "Marcus, if you're involved with Jenna and the agency finds out, you may have some real problems."

"Brady! What brought that on? And you have got to be kidding. On our first assignment, they teamed us as newlyweds. We hardly knew each other. That more or less tells me they were encouraging involvement."

"I'm afraid not, Marcus. The agency doesn't think that way. You are teamed together to do an assignment. There is a basic rule. You can never become involved with your partner."

"Brady, you've got to be bullshitting me."

"Marcus, that's just the way it is. The agency just feels that involvement can compromise your decision-making in dangerous situations. That's their thought. If they find out you are involved, one of you could get fired or at the least you would never be teamed together. I got this lecture when I was involved with Martina's mother. It might've been years ago, but I'm sure it still applies.

Look, all I can say is if you are, or you're thinking about getting involved, don't. If you do, do everything you can to keep it from the agency. You must maintain the appearance that you're nothing more than a good working team. Partners, not lovers."

After that exchange they both went back to work on their respective computers. Marcus, however, began to think again about Jenna and his potential relationship. *Yes, we experienced an assignment together as a team that involved 11 days of living together on a cruise ship. Prior to that, I really had no relationship with her even though we worked in the same office. Immediately following the cruise, she was badly hurt by an explosion we both experienced entering a condo owned by the Gambioni family. She ended up in the hospital and I was immediately transferred to the MI6 in the UK. I really haven't seen or spoken to her until a few days ago when she came to San Gimignano. Yes, we became quite close on that cruise; and yes, we slept together, but that was quite a while ago. She obviously has feelings for me. What really are my feelings for her? Do I really want to be with her just for comfort because we both lost close friends or do I want to be with her because I have strong feelings for her?*

If Brady is right, maybe I should try to stave off any future involvement with her and try to just be friends and a partner. If we get assigned together again, that may be difficult because really right now I can only think of holding her.

These thoughts continued to bounce around in Marcus's head for the remainder of the flight with no clear resolution. They receded to the back of his mind as they started their approach into New York.

"Brady, luckily it's clear. Look out the window. Manhattan sure looks great," said Marcus. "It's only been a few months but it feels like I have been away a long time. We will be on final approach into LaGuardia in just a few minutes and I just can't wait to get there. It's been exciting and an emotional adventure, been to places I never dreamed I would get to. But there's no place like home."

"Amen to that!" said Brady.

CHAPTER 13

New York, New York

It was a little past noon in New York when the Gulfstream taxied to the CIA hanger on the civil side of LaGuardia. The hanger doors were open and parked out front were two SUVs and a black Honda sedan. With her blonde flowing hair and a white jacket, Jenna stood out among the ground crew that were assembled in front of the vehicles.

"Well, we have a greeting party," said Marcus, peering out the window of the Gulfstream.

"Yes, and it's nice to see it doesn't include armed soldiers like we witnessed in the airports in Europe," said Brady.

As they both deplaned Brady called out to the techs who were opening the luggage compartment, "The bags with the red tags are mine. The others are Marcus's."

Jenna rushed up, threw her arms around Marcus, saying, "Welcome home," and followed with a long romantic kiss.

Standing by, Brady commented, "Wow, that's quite a welcome. Hello, Jenna. I don't think we met before."

"No, I don't believe so either, but welcome home," she said, shaking his hand and then giving him a hug.

"Tell the SUV drivers where you want your luggage delivered and then come join me in the Honda. I hope you ate on the trip over as you are scheduled for a meeting at 2:00 p.m.. Initially they want a combined briefing after which you will be broken off to brief your respective mission leaders. I will be going with you, Marcus. With the traffic we have to deal with, we will just about make it."

Within a short time their bags were loaded in the SUVs and Marcus and Brady hopped in the car with Jenna. After the usual small talk, such as how was the trip, was the flight smooth, etc., Jenna began to relate an interesting story. "While you both have been traveling home," she said, "the last 48 hours in the US has been quite active. First, based on the information you provided us and we provided the FBI, they found where the shipping containers were being delivered and the facility where the cocaine-impregnated wine was being shipped and processed. They made a raid and it wasn't pleasant. There was a shootout and in addition to the Gambioni crime family members, Angelina was there and a stray bullet killed her. That wasn't planned at all. Of course, crime family word travels fast and Franco heard about the raid. Even though figuratively Angelina was running the family, there is no question, Franco, though in prison, was calling the shots. The word on the street is, when he heard his daughter was killed, he hung himself in his cell that night. When I left for the airport, headquarters had not yet verified this but I'm sure they will have answers when we get back. Marcus, it appears your vengeance on the Gambioni family has been accomplished."

At that point there was complete silence in the car for several minutes. Then Brady spoke up, saying, "Was there any word on what happened in Italy when they raided the vineyard in Tuscany?"

"I haven't heard but I'm sure at the combined briefing we will get whatever they have heard from either the Italian government or MI6," responded Jenna.

Marcus then spoke up, saying, "You know, as much as I wished the worst on Franco, and no question, he was a ruthless criminal, I can't help feeling a little sorry for him. The shock of losing Angelina would be crushing. Though she certainly was as ruthless as her father, she was an extremely attractive and vivacious young lady. But she was also smart, capable, and cunning, a martial arts expert and schooled in all aspects available and exploited by organized crime today."

Then reaching over and placing his hand on Jenna's knee he said, "Jenna, I believe that wraps up both our first and second assignments. In my mind I think we can consider ourselves experienced agents and ready for whatever the agency has in store for us."

Brady then commented, "I totally agree. Welcome to the operational world of the CIA."

⊕

Both Marcus and Jenna returned to their original job, running background investigations on foreign delegates to the UN. This was the standard assignment that agents in the New York office were given between operational assignments.

Shortly after their return, Leo's parents in the northern England invited them for a visit, all-expenses-paid, as they wished to have a firsthand knowledge of their son's life in his final days.

In appreciation of their visit, Leo's parents took them to local sites, including Hadrian's Wall and Gretna Green. One can only speculate what happened on the visit to the Old Blacksmiths Shop in Gretna Green where the old Smithy Marriage Anvil resides. Needless to say, the smile on their faces remained throughout their stay and their trip home.

The End.

EPILOGUE

"**M**arcus, Jenna, report!" The PA system boomed across the cubicles on the tenth floor of the CIA office complex in Manhattan. Some things change and some things never do. Marcus and Jenna had adjoining cubicles; their boss had made it clear he could care less about their relationship. All he concerned himself with was their performance. However, he still loved the PA system rather than a phone, much to the chagrin of the staff.

"Marcus, Jenna, now!" boomed the PA system again. They both rapidly got up, nearly colliding as they exited their cubicles and rushed to the boss's office. "Close the door, sit." said the boss. "Did you enjoy the UK? Are you married? Not that it makes a difference," he continued in his usual crisp tone.

"Well, we did visit . . ." Marcus started to respond.

"Both of you. Relax and listen. You both will be teamed on a new operational assignment. Again, you will be under cover and teamed as a young married couple. However, in preparation, you both are to report to the Presidio in Monterey, California. There you will attend the Defense Language Institute Foreign Language Center. You will report there next Monday. You will be schooled in Mandarin Chinese and Malay. Now go. Make your travel arrangements."

Before you close the book.

I sincerely hope you enjoyed the story as much as I enjoyed writing it. Jenna and Marcus are destined to have further adventures, and I will do my best to bring them to you.

I, as all writers, wish to get our stories into the hands of as many readers as possible. Therefore, it's critical for you to write a review. It can be as brief as a couple of words or several sentences. But please, now go onto Amazon and write a review.

Thank you.
Larry Andrews

www.larryandrewsnovelist.com